Drivin' Me Crazy

Joan Conning Afman

A Wings ePress, Inc
Romantic Comedy Novel

Wings ePress, Inc.

Edited by: Jeanne Smith
Copy Edited by: Joan C. Powell
Executive Editor: Jeanne Smith
Cover Artist: Trisha FitzGerald-Jung

All rights reserved

Wings ePress Books
www.wingsepress.com

Copyright © 2019 by: Joan Conning Afman
ISBN-13: 978-1-61309-597-3
ISBN-10: 1-61309-597-X

Published In the United States Of America

Wings ePress Inc.
3000 N. Rock Road
Newton, KS 67114

Dedication

To Carla Brind and Rita Hazen, who have always encouraged
my writing and painting.

* * *

One

"Here he comes, right on time."

Raina looked up from her computer and exchanged a knowing glance with her friend, Marisol. Sure enough, Duff's lanky frame appeared in the door of her cubicle.

"Good morning, beautiful one."

Raina sighed and attempted a smile in his direction. "Hello, Duff. What's on your intellectual mind this morning?"

With a flourish, he pulled two tickets from his shirt pocket. "The Russian Ballet at the Kravis!" He looked at them as if they were made of pure gold. "Saturday night, okay?"

Marisol slid between them. "Excuse me, Duff. I need to get back to my own desk."

"And you're looking very attractive yourself, Miss Martinez." Duff gave her a courtly bow and stepped aside to let her pass.

"Thanks," she threw behind her as she scurried down the corridor.

Raina looked after her. "She likes you, you know. You ought to ask her out."

With an exaggerated gesture, he clapped a hand across his heart. "She's not the fair maiden who lives in here. You are, Raina."

"I know," she shot back. "But I think my lease is over. I'd like a chance to move out."

He laughed, reached over and ruffled her hair. "Well done. I love your sense of humor. Now how about the ballet?"

Annoyed, she pulled her head away. "Duff, I just don't know how to discourage you. I'm not the girl for you. I don't like all that cultural stuff. I'm a bowling addict; I like to sit in a bar, sip a beer and watch sports on TV. I watch *Jeopardy,* and wouldn't miss any of those real housewife shows. I love the Kardashians." She ran out of breath, stopped, and looked up at him. "I even stopped wearing makeup, whether you noticed or not, hoping you'd find me less attractive. Look at what I'm wearing!" She picked at the fabric of her khaki-colored shirt which she'd paired with plain black pants. "I dress in the most boring things in my closet, hoping you'll find me boring. Duff, you're driving me crazy! What do I have to do to turn you off?"

He looked bewildered. "You want me to find you boring? That's never going to happen, Raina. You're so naturally beautiful you don't need makeup anyway, and I love those simple clothes." He swept a hand around, indicating the whole of the office complex. "Those overdressed girls with their fancy hair-dos and trashy jewelry all look cheap. I prefer the real thing." He stepped back and regarded her with a wide grin. "You. You are the real thing, and you are perfect. Like the Mona Lisa."

She put her head in her hands. "Oh, puh-leeze! Don't waste your art analogies on me. I'm just not into it, and I never know what you're talking about anyway.

They both looked up as they heard the office manager's high heels click on the tiled floor. Dianne Ryder skidded to an abrupt halt, and looked from Duff to Raina and back again, frowning. She tilted her chin into the air. "Miss Hudson, may I see you and Miss Martinez in my office in about ten minutes?"

"Of course, Miss Ryder." Raina glared at Duff and gave him a nudge of her chin, hoping to send him the message to be on his way.

"And, you, Mr. Duffy. I assume you have work to do?"

Duff lifted his chin at the same angle as hers, and glanced at his watch. "I've been here since nine o'clock. I assume I have ten minutes for a morning break, and I have one minute left."

"Then I assume you will use it to get back to your cubicle." Dianne switched her gaze to Raina. "Ten minutes." She swept on down the hall, her back straight as a board, her dark French-twisted hair the last thing they saw as she disappeared around the corner."

"Whew!" Raina breathed. "I can't believe you can talk back to her like that. Everyone else is scared stiff of her. Those eerie blue eyes of hers are like darts of icy fire when she looks at you."

"I assume," Duff said, "that I will not be here that long. I'm certainly not going to make a career out of working here, and neither should you. I'm getting responses to my resumè. One of these days I'll be teaching art history somewhere in the rarified air of a college, and this place will be just a memory."

"I wish you well," Raina said, meaning it. A new job for Duff would get him out of her hair for good. But she also felt the slightest jab of regret. She would miss him. What? She would miss him? Forget about it!

He leaned over the cubicle partition and fixed his eyes on her. "That's why it's really important, Raina, that we cement our relationship. I want you to go with me. You deserve better than this." He grinned at her. "You're driving me crazy too, Raina, and I love it."

"What?" She couldn't believe her ears. Was he proposing?"

"So, I'll pick you up at five on Saturday. We'll go someplace nice for dinner."

She sighed in defeat then reluctantly agreed. She liked him, but it could never work between them. The differences, intellectual and cultural, were just too great. She always felt as if she were trying to leap over a wide crevice in the ground in order to catch up with him. She sighed. "Not a French restaurant, please. All those sauces and herbs—I'm just not a fancy eater."

He winked. "We'll play it by eye."

She smiled in spite of herself. "I wish you wouldn't say that. You know it's 'play it by ear'."

"Yeah, but I'm a visual person. For me it's play it by eye. Five o'clock then?"

"I assume so," she said, turning back to her computer. She heard the click of Dianne's heels, returning from wherever she had gone.

"Do you know," Duff whispered in a conspiratorial tone, "that when you assume anything, you make an ass of u and me?" He winked again, with the other eye, and started back down the corridor.

How does he do that? I can only wink with my left eye, not my right. Well, that's Duff. He's different, that's for sure.

Her eyes followed him as he went back to his cubicle. He must have checked his email, and everyone turned to look at him, as he said, loud enough for everyone to hear, "Another message from Tanya. Can't she get it through her head that our relationship is over. As in O-V-E-R?"

~ * ~

Dianne sat behind her nastily-neat desk, and motioned to the two girls to take seats. They sat. She adjusted her glasses, then without preamble said, "Your request for a two-week vacation has been approved."

"Thank you," they said in unison, like well-behaved school children.

She wasn't finished, of course. "You realize this will put a lot of pressure on the other employees, with both of you gone at the same time. Mr. Duffy will really have to up his game."

"I'm sure he's capable of that," Marisol said. They started to rise, but Dianne held up her hand. "I'd like a word with Miss Hudson, please."

Marisol threw a sympathetic glance at Raina, and left the office, closing the door carefully behind her. Dianne had actually been known to write up an employee who closed her office door too hard. The poor girl had been forced to sit alone in one of the conference rooms and listen to a long lecture on tape about respecting one's office superiors, and 'appropriate office etiquette.'

Raina gazed at Dianne, trying to swallow the apprehension she felt. Was she being terminated, and if so—what for?"

"Miss Ryder—" she began.

Dianne waved her quiet. "Not about your work, Miss Hudson, which is, let's say, adequate."

It would kill her to give anyone a compliment!

Dianne's pale blue eyes raked over her, making her feel as though the temperature had dropped twenty degrees. "This is about your appearance. It seems to have...shall we say, gone downhill in the past few weeks." She indicated Raina's khaki shirt. "What you're wearing today, for instance, looks more suitable for washing your car than for the office."

Raina gasped. She couldn't believe her ears.

"And what happened to your hair and your makeup?"

"Well...I—" Raina couldn't find the words. How could she tell Dianne she was trying to discourage Michael Duffy's unwanted attentions?

Dianne parted her lips in what might have been interpreted as a smile. "Well, Miss Hudson, when you first started working here, I was impressed with your sense of style and overall appearance. I felt you were a good candidate to move up the line in the office hierarchy. But—" again the ice blue eyes flicked over her. "It is crucial to keep to a high standard of dress, also. I don't know why you're letting yourself go, but I expect since I've called it to your attention, you will now attend to the situation." She turned to her computer and began to type.

Raina sat frozen to her chair.

Dianne's eyes were the only thing that moved, as they surveyed Raina one more time. "That's all. You may go."

Raina stumbled out of the office, making sure to close the door quietly behind her.

Marisol waited in her cubicle. She sat in Raina's chair, biting her fingernails. "Well, what did she want?"

Raina slumped against the wall. "It's a wonder she doesn't freeze to death and turn into some sort of ice sculpture that only Duff could appreciate!"

Marisol jumped up and helped Raina sit down. "What? What did she say?"

Raina gulped and wiped a tear from her eye. "That I was neglecting my appearance, and killing my chances for advancement, and she wants me to dress the way I used to when I first started working here."

"My God! Did she really have the nerve to comment on your clothes?"

"She said I'm dressed like I would be washing my car."

Marisol choked down a laugh. "She didn't!"

"She did." Raina snatched a Kleenex from the box on her desk and blew her nose. "At least we have our vacation time. I'll be so glad to get away from here and Dictator Dianne for two weeks."

~ * ~

Raina watched as Duff flew out of Dianne's office at four-thirty that afternoon, and stormed directly to Raina's cubicle. She sat back and looked up at him. No avoiding the issue now. "I gather she told you, and you're not happy about the extra work you're going to have to do while we're gone, right?"

He blew out through his lips. "A monkey could do the work. I spend three-quarters of my time at the computer on my desk writing a novel about Marc Chagall, the other quarter doing my job, and I have time left over. Why didn't you tell me you and Marisol were taking two weeks' vacation? Where are you going?"

She sighed. "I didn't tell you for this very reason, Duff. I didn't want you getting upset, getting protective, telling me I can't go."

He leaned over the rail. "No, I don't want you to go at all, but if you've already made arrangements, I hope it's a group tour with plenty of protection."

She met his eyes with a challenging glare. "We're not taking any kind of tour."

He leaned in closer. "Are you going on a cruise, then? You won't be running around on those islands by yourself, will you? That can be dangerous."

"No, we're not going on a cruise. And, Duff, I really don't have to tell you what our plans are."

A hurt look flicked across his face, and she relented a little. "We'll be okay. Two weeks and we'll be right back here on the job."

He thought for a moment, then seemed to have a burst of inspiration, and his face brightened. "Oh! You're going to visit someone...friends, relatives? You're flying to a different part of the country? I hope it's not one of those big cities, New York or Chicago. You never can tell—"

She almost laughed. He really was rather endearing, but... "Duff!"

He stopped and looked at her, and she saw what she had hoped not to see reflected in his eyes. He loved her. He had never said it in so many words, but his constant attention to her, his compliments, his refusal to take 'no' for an answer when he asked her out, the money he spent on her...now she saw it, plain as day. He was in love with her. But—it could never work. She didn't love him. She liked him, felt a certain physical attraction that she didn't want to feel...but, well, it just could never work out between them. Their backgrounds and interests were just too different.

She took a deep breath and said the words she knew he'd hate. "Marisol and I are just going on a driving trip by ourselves. We don't have any firm plans made. We're just going to drive around for a week, then we'll turn around and take another route back. We want to see some other regions of the country."

He turned so pale she thought he might faint. She reached out to him. "Duff...!"

He waved his hands over his head. "You can't do that! That's not safe for two young girls to be doing. I forbid you to even think of doing that! If you must go, take a tour with other people. Go on a cruise! Driving around by yourselves is way too dangerous. Do you know how many lunatics are out there, and people with guns driving around and just waiting for—"

She held up her hand. "You can't forbid me! What kind of last century word is that, anyway! What kind of last century attitude? This is what we want to do, and we're going to do it."

He looked so comical, standing there, helpless and unhappy, that she felt a shaft of sympathy for him. She shouldn't laugh at him for caring so much about her.

"It's too dangerous! There are predators out there, just looking for women on their own to take advantage of. Rapists, robbers, murderers. Drive-by shootings. The news is full of women molested and abducted every night. Please don't do this."

"And plenty of women arrive home every night with nothing happening to them. For heaven's sake, Duff, we're not giddy teenagers. We have common sense. We have cell phones. We'll be careful."

His whole body seemed to droop. She looked at him, truly sorry to be causing him unhappiness, and saw with shock that there were tears in his clear blue eyes.

She laid her hand on his. He looked down at their hands together. He turned his hand over and held hers, and put his other hand over both of them. He looked absolutely miserable. "How could I go on living if something happened to you?"

She withdrew her hand, but made her voice gentle. "Nothing's going to happen to me, Duff—but you have to let go of whatever illusions you have of us as a couple. There's not going to be a future for you and me." She raised her eyes to his. "I really feel awful saying this, but I just don't feel the same as you do. We're not suited to each other."

"You mean the cultural stuff?" he asked. "If you'd just give it a chance, Raina, you'd start to see how the arts enrich your life. You'd start to feel it."

"I haven't felt anything in those art galleries you've dragged me through," she countered, "except sore feet. Ditto for the concerts I could hardly stay awake through. I like words with my music. I can't tell an oboe from a clarinet, and I doubt I ever will." She rolled her eyes. "As for that opera—I had nightmares for weeks. I'd much rather go see a B-minus movie."

"But—how about the ballet Saturday? You will go with me, won't you?"

She regarded him with a steady gaze and hardened her heart. "Yes, but, Duff, this comes with a condition."

"What? Anything!"

"By the time Marisol and I get back from our trip, I want you to have dated at least two other girls. You're wasting your time on me. Is it a deal?"

"Oh, Raina. There just isn't anyone else for me."

"I won't go to the ballet unless you promise me that. Two dates with other girls."

He hesitated. "Raina, you're drivin' me crazy! Well, okay, two dates. But I'm not going to enjoy them."

Two

Friday morning Duff came in late and headed straight for Dianne's office. He didn't even look at Raina as he walked by her desk, shoulders bent and head down.

"What the—?" Marisol, sharing her morning coffee and office gossip with Raina, looked after him. "What's up with him?"

"He's probably going to complain about the two-date ultimatum I gave him yesterday," Raina joked. She took a sip of her coffee.

Marisol giggled. "You're so mean. I think he's really a great guy— kinda dorky, but cute, and smart. I'd love to go out with him, but I can't stay here and be one of his two dates if I'm on the road with you."

Raina shook her head. "I'd love it if you went out with him. Get him off my case." She felt Marisol's gaze on her.

Raina turned her head toward her. "What?"

Marisol set her coffee cup on Raina's desk and put her hand on her friend's arm. Her voice took on a more serious tone. "You know, Raina, Duff's really a great catch. You don't know how lucky you are to have a guy like that interested in you. You could do a lot worse. Why not try to take him seriously? You like him, why not see if you can love him like he loves you?"

Raina shook her head. "I'm a blue-collar girl at heart, Mare. All those high-brow things he likes to do, they just leave me cold."

"He took you to the Norton a couple weeks ago. How did that go?"

Raina spread her palms. "How do you think it went? Over my head, that's where. He explains and explains and I still don't get it. Like that glass maker, what's his name, Cha—something?"

"Chihuly?"

"Yeah. Well, at the Norton they have this room that has a ceiling he supposedly made, or his students or apprentices or something. You lie on a black leather bench and look up at it. It's supposed to be like looking up from the bottom of the ocean, at least I think that's what Duff said it meant."

"And what did it look like to you?"

Raina shrugged. "Like somebody threw a lot of pieces of colored glass in a bowl of gelatin, and I was drowning in it. I don't get it. Why is this guy famous for freaking making things out of glass?"

Marisol laughed. "Why shouldn't he, if he wants to?"

Heated up, Raina continued. "And then there's that Gertrude O'Keeffe."

Marisol smiled. "Georgia."

"Whatever. Duff said her paintings are of flowers 'way up close, so they look like caverns you could walk into, but they're really symbolic paintings of women's genitals." She put her hands on her hips and glared at Marisol. "Now tell me, why would someone paint a flower so up close that you can't tell what it looks like? And if you want a picture of a cavern, paint a cavern! And as for the last part of that, well…" she shook her head, at a loss for words. "It all just doesn't make any sense to me."

"Maybe if you took a course in art history," Marisol suggested.

"That's what Duff is going to teach, if he ever gets a job. If I can't understand it when he explains it, why would I be able to learn it from somebody else?"

Marisol was about to answer, but snapped her mouth shut as Dianne's office door opened with a rush. The office manager stormed out, her face like a dark cloud, with Duff right behind her.

"You!" Dianne jabbed two fingers at Raina and Marisol. "To Conference Room Two at mega-speed. Get a wiggle on. Now!'

She clicked-clicked around the corner of the corridor before the two girls managed to exit the cubicle. They dashed after her and Duff's retreating back.

Dianne had already seated herself at the head of the long, oval table, and was tapping her pen impatiently on the tabletop as they entered the room.

Duff circled around in back of her and claimed a seat on her right, closer to the center of the table. Raina and Marisol took chairs on her left, opposite Duff.

Dianne glared at them all, then fixed her pale blue stare on Raina. "Miss Hudson, just what are you three trying to pull here?"

Raina felt the heat rise to her cheeks. "Trying to pull?" she repeated, mystified. "I'm sorry, Miss Ryder, but I don't know what you're talking about."

"Oh, don't you?" Up went Dianne's chin, as she looked down her nose at her. "If I recall rightly, you and Miss Martinez are both leaving for vacation on Monday, and will be gone for two weeks. Isn't that so?"

Raina nodded, feeling like a limp dishrag. "Yes. We've had that time okayed by both you and Personnel for a long time."

"That's right," Marisol put in.

Dianne rose from her chair, planted her manicured hands on the table, and leaned forward, causing all three to jerk backwards, although there were at least four feet between her and them. "Do you think I do not know things that happen around this office? Do you think I do not know that the three of you are tight friends...that you, Miss Hudson, and you, Mr. Duffy frequently date? That you, Miss Martinez, are Miss Hudson's best friend, and also very friendly with Mr. Duffy?"

Out of breath, Dianne sat back again, and everyone else returned to their previous positions.

Raina looked across the table and caught Duff's eyes. He had not yet said a word, and, unusual for him, he wore a tired and rather drained expression. What in the world was going on with him? Was just the thought of her trip sucking the very life from him? "Well, yes, Miss Ryder, Duff and I do date, and Marisol is my best friend. But—that's not against company policy, is it? I'm very confused as to why this is a problem."

"That is not the problem," Dianne snapped. "The problem, young lady, is that when three people whom I know to be very close friends will all be gone from the office at the same time, and for the same length of time, it puts a considerable strain on the work load around here."

Raina raised her eyebrows and looked at Duff. "Are you taking the next two weeks off, too, Duff?"

He nodded, knit his brows, looked down at the table, and traced the wood grain with an idle finger. "My grandmother died. In Maine. I have to go there and help the family with funeral arrangements."

"And you have to be gone for two weeks?" Marisol asked.

Duff nodded, his face so drawn and serious that Raina almost thought he might be faking the entire scenario, just to be gone when they were gone. But, no—he was so conscientious. He wouldn't pull a stunt like that, would he?

"My mom called late last night. It was very sudden. Granny wasn't sick or anything. We—our family wasn't even that close to her after my father died—but she made me the executor of her will—and well, Mom says it's a mess, and the lawyer says I have to be there to help straighten things out." He shrugged. "Believe me, this isn't anything I want to do, but...my mom needs me to go up there and help her handle things."

Raina narrowed her eyes and searched his face for any sign of untruth, but didn't detect anything. But this was a very strange coincidence, wasn't it? Was he intending to follow her and Marisol on their road trip? But, no—Duff wouldn't do that, would he? That would be stalking. Would he?

Dianne pursed her lips. "And you figure this will take two weeks." Her tone was frigid.

Not the least intimidated, Duff nodded. "That's what the lawyer suggested we would need, yes."

Dianne bore down on the pen so hard it suddenly snapped in two. She gave it a baleful look, and returned her attention to Raina and Marisol. "Then, for the good of the company, you two will have to postpone your vacation. Mr. Duffy does a lot of work around here, more than you two put together, actually, and we simply can't operate with all three of you gone."

She stood, as if the conference were over and her decision final.

"No!" Raina and Marisol said in unison.

Dianne froze in her tracks and turned an equally frigid look on each of them. "What do you mean, no?"

"We have tickets for things," Marisol attempted to explain. "Tickets for Disneyworld, and they're already paid for. We've reserved places at an event in St. Augustine—"

"Ah, an event," Duff breathed. Raina shot him a dirty look.

"And a reservation for a tour in Savannah that you have to make *months* in advance, and tickets for...well, other things that are just about impossible to get, and dates can't be changed—"

"Other things," Duff breathed, raising his eyes to the ceiling, as if he'd had a glimpse of heaven.

Raina controlled her amusement. He really was very funny sometimes! And he didn't seem averse to using his humor to infuriate Dianne. Well, good for him.

"Yes, other things," Marisol finished. "Plus we have motel and hotel reservations. There's just no way we can change our plans. Can't you get temp help?"

Dianne held up her wrist and cast a meaningful look at her watch. "And just where am I supposed to get temp help at five o'clock on a Friday afternoon?"

Raina had a sudden idea. "Mrs. Ryder, I have a cousin who does office work as a temp. She was just telling me she had nothing lined up for the next week or so. She's really good—do you want me to ask her to come in?"

"Drop off her name and phone number on my desk before you leave," Dianne snapped. "But the three of you, take note, I am not thrilled with any of this." She paused to look Raina over from head to toe, perusing with her icy blue eyes the tailored gray suit and pink blouse Raina wore. "But I do note, Miss Hudson, that you paid attention to my advice regarding your appearance. Much better. I approve."

She turned on her heel and whisked from the room.

"Whew!" Marisol brushed back her long dark hair with her hand. "That was no fun." She turned to Duff. "I'm so sorry about your grandmother."

He looked at her blankly. "What?" He caught himself. "Yes, well she was ninety-two. Or three. We all have to go sometime. I really don't look forward to doing this, but it's my mom I'm really concerned about. She's a wreck."

All three stood to leave. Duff came around the table, put his hands on Raina's shoulders and gave her a long, soulful look. "I'll pick you up tomorrow at five, my Mona Lisa." He straightened up and walked off, the same way he'd been shuffling around the office all day long.

Three

For her dinner-ballet date with Duff, Raina chose a simple, short blue halter dress and her highest high heels with silver with skinny straps that wound around her ankles. At the last moment she added the sterling silver hand-made dangling earrings he had given her on her last birthday. She sighed as she viewed herself in the mirror. She didn't even know *that girl*!

Right on time as usual, Duff picked her up in his ancient black Toyota, and drove to the restaurant.

She had been there before, and it was a restaurant she loved. They offered fancy fare on the menu, yes, but they also had plain good old American food well-cooked. Lots of seafood. Maybe she could even have a clam roll, though Duff would roll his eyes when she ordered it.

They sat on the deck of the pink stucco lodge-like building, which looked out over the ocean in the distance.

She loved Florida. Southern-born and raised, she hoped she'd never have to live in that cold, distant north, where she'd never even visited. It sounded so intimidating, from what her several friends who'd moved there told her. Winters so cold they thought they'd never be warm again. Driving on the slippery, ice-covered streets was like a self-invitation to disaster. Spring was one beautiful day in April, followed by days of rain, cold temps one day, hot the next, so you could never plan what to wear. You needed a lot of clothes there, not just a wardrobe of shorts and tees and a few work and dress clothes. In summer you could count the blue-sky days on one hand. It rained a lot in summer, too, and not just a quick storm, as in Florida, followed by the sun coming out and smiling on the tanned inhabitants again in an hour or two. Long, gray days, one after another. She shivered. It sounded awful.

Floridians who had been there said autumn was beautiful, though. The trees were unbelievably glorious when their leaves turned all those gorgeous colors. But they felt as though the mountains hemmed them in, and the trees were horrendously tall and full, almost threatening.

Duff interrupted her thoughts. "What are you thinking?"

She smiled. "How I love Florida."

"New England's pretty special, too. Our country began there, you know. Are you familiar with the work of the Hudson River painters?"

She sighed. "No. And the Hudson River's in New York state, isn't it?" She really wasn't sure, but she'd heard Hudson River and New York City linked before.

"Grandma Moses, alias Anna Mary Robertson?"

"Oh, that's the lady who can't even draw. How did she get famous?"

Duff smiled. "She could draw, but it's called a 'primitive' style. It has its own charm."

She shrugged. "I like my pictures to look real, the way they should."

He gave her a tolerant smile. "Realism isn't necessarily what art is all about. But someday your eyes will open and you will really learn to see."

For some reason, his remark didn't raise her hackles in annoyance, as it often did. What did he mean, really learn to see? Was there some secret that people who were so in love with art knew that others didn't? The thought only lingered a moment, then like a sudden itch, vanished.

"I can see fine now," she quipped, "and I see our dinner coming."

The waiter arrived with her clam roll and steak fries, and Duff's order of a stew-like dish he said was famous in New Orleans. She looked at it and gave an inward shudder. He was welcome to it. It was just like those paintings he was so crazy about; you couldn't tell what the heck was in there.

"So exactly where are you from?" she asked. "New England, I know, but what town or city?" She wondered to herself why she had never asked him.

"Stockbridge, Mass," he said, putting down his fork. "There's a museum there that features another important artist, Norman Rockwell. He's very realistic, in his own way, famous for his *Saturday Evening Post* covers. I think you'd like his paintings."

"Maybe," she said, not wanting to commit herself to liking any art she hadn't seen a sample of. And the *Saturday Evening Post* was well before her time.

"I'll take you there someday," he said, and dug into his pile of unidentifiable food again.

She gave an inward sigh. *No you won't, Duff. I'm not going.* Then a little prickle of curiosity tweaked her. Wouldn't she like to see New England, tour it with someone like Duff who was so crazy about the area and so knowledgeable about it? She took a bite of her clam roll. Delicious. And Maine was famous for its lobster, wasn't it? She loved lobster.

After dinner, in spite of her reservations, Raina became caught up in the beauty of the ballet. Seated in the plush seat of the grand old art deco-inspired theatre, she glanced around. Everyone was so well-dressed, looked so sophisticated. In spite of herself, a sinking feeling of self-doubt began to overwhelm her. Who was she, raised in a simple, almost shabby Latino neighborhood, to be sitting here, bordered on the sides and front and back by impeccably-dressed, sophisticated looking people?

What did Duff see in her anyway?

The woman sitting next to Raina, twenty years older by her estimation, one of those garden-club ladies who probably sat on half a dozen important boards, wearing a dress that obviously bore a designer label, turned to her and smiled. "You're looking absolutely lovely tonight. Only you younger gals can wear a dress and shoes like that. Perfect on you."

Astonished out of her self-doubting reverie, Raina could only stammer, "Thank you." She glanced at Duff, who said nothing, but his beaming face told it all.

The movements of the dancers were so graceful, so incredible, she couldn't understand how a human body could get into some of those positions. The costumes were exquisite in their design, fabrics and colors, and the music—even without words—swept over her, catching her up in the fairy-tale world of the captivating performance.

She felt Duff watching her, and she turned her head to catch his eye.

He grinned at her, leaned over and whispered, "You've never seen a live ballet, have you?"

She shook her head, not trusting herself to answer. The entire experience was overwhelming, but there was no way she was going to admit that to him. It would just encourage him to keep 'educating' her in the arts, and she didn't want that. She liked her life the way it was. This was her first, and her last, ballet.

Something inside seemed to shift and Raina knew she was on the verge of a big change in her life if she did not protect the one she had. And she thought she preferred her life the way she lived it now: her blue-collar parents, her best-friend from grammar school, Marisol, the beers with pals at the local club, traditional Latino foods, her ethnic neighborhood, people she understood who understood her. No, she didn't want anything else, and she could not conceive at all that it could be richer, deeper...more. Her life was fine, just the way it was.

Yes, she'd have to keep Duff at arm's length when they all returned to the office. That's not to say she wouldn't miss him, she thought wistfully. He was so gentle, so thoughtful, unlike most of the guys she had dated. And, after their dates, when he put his arms around her and kissed her, she often forgot he wasn't the one for her, and it was hard to pull away. But—she had often asked herself—wasn't that just the man-woman thing acting up? She had physical needs like anyone else, and sometimes she felt herself getting carried away, forgot that it was Duff, the cultural nerd, who was kissing her. Maybe, if she were lucky, one of the colleges would give him a job starting in the fall. And if it were far enough away, like in New England, that would solve the problem for her.

He caught her hand, intertwining his long fingers with hers as they left the Kravis. "Have you ever been here?"

She shook her head and pulled her hand away, refusing to acknowledge the tingle that ran through her at his touch. "I told you a thousand times that my family just wasn't into this sort of thing, and I never had the urge to go either."

"But did you enjoy it?"

She shrugged. "Well, now I can tell everyone I've been here. But I saw those ticket prices when we went in—you could see ten movies for what it cost to see that ballet."

"Oh, Raina, Raina," he said. "Why did I have to fall in love with you?"

"I wish you hadn't," she said, forcing a chill into her voice.

He left her at her family's home. She didn't invite him in. He looked at her with longing in his eyes, then put his arms around her and hugged her close. "You be ultra-careful on that trip," he breathed into her ear. He pulled away slightly, bent and placed a light kiss on her lips. He turned, and with his long, awkward stride, returned to his car, backed out of the driveway and gave her a quick wave as he drove away.

She watched the car disappear into the night, and felt a tiny shaft of guilt. She had enjoyed the ballet. It was an experience to go to the Kravis Center, and she hadn't even given him the satisfaction of knowing that.

And, she thought, as she unlocked the door, she'd never once asked him about the death of his grandmother.

Four

Duff, who lived across town from Raina, thought of her starting out on her car trip with Marisol and shuddered. He was filled with apprehension, but he knew there was nothing he could do to stop them.

Impatiently, he threw a few basic articles of clothing and underwear into his tattered suitcase. This grandmother, Norah Tyler, had never been part of his life. He barely remembered her. Although a native Stockbridgian, if that's a word, after the death of his paternal grandfather, she had remarried, moved to a remote section of Maine. Duff's father had followed his dad into an early demise, and Grandma Tyler had never visited them in Stockbridge, or even communicated with them, except for an occasional Christmas card.

Apparently, his mother had told him, the funeral arrangements had been taken care of. But he needed to be there to sign documents, to take over ownership of the house and a brand-new Lexus, to decide what he wanted to do with them.

"OK," he had agreed, but he felt a sudden lilt in his heart, and a shaft of gratitude to Norah Tyler. His thoughts spun around a like a child's top on the sidewalk. He hadn't even known Grandma Tyler, but she had left him a house and a car. He would sell the house, but he would have the means to put a good deposit down on something for him and Raina once he got his teaching position.

"I'll fly up. Can you pick me up in Albany, or Hartford, and we'll drive up from there?"

She surprised him by asking, "Do you still have that old blue Chevy?"

"It's an old black Toyota," he replied, "but yeah, I do—but I don't want to drive that all the way up there. I thought I'd fly up, you could drive us up to Maine, and I'll take possession of the Lexus there."

"And what will you do with your old one, the Toyota?"

He shrugged, even though he knew she couldn't see that. "I dunno. Sell it on line for whatever I can get for it, I guess."

"It's still in good shape, isn't it?"

"Well, sure, I take care of it—but why shouldn't I fly? I won't need a car while I'm there, if you're there, too."

His mother's voice floated over the line. "I have a request, Duff. I need your car. I want you to drive it up and leave it here."

"Why?" He couldn't comprehend that. Why would she need his old car? If she needed a vehicle, she could well afford to buy one.

"It's essentially a piece of junk," Duff protested. "I'd be lucky to get a few hundred for it."

"Grandma Gray is involved in a new program at church. We help people who are down and out find jobs, and if someone has an old car to donate, we give them that, too, when they get a job."

Grandma Gray. Unlike the remote Maine grandmother, Victoria Gray had lived all her life in Stockbridge. At seventy-five she was as alive and productive as anyone he'd ever known. And as far as he knew, she'd never set foot in Maine. She was one of those women whose ancestors had settled the town she lived in, and she saw no reason to leave it, ever. A visit to Pittsfield was lowering her standards, and a trip to New York City...well, that was a safari to a pagan land.

He adored her, though. Victoria Gray had spoiled him rotten when his mother was not around, read to him, taught him songs—mostly old hymns—played chess, checkers and Scrabble with him—

she always won, and taught him how to cook. They had a special bond, and he was anxious to see her again, and ever so glad she wasn't the grandmother who had died. But what did she need with his car? That didn't make any sense at all.

Duff rubbed his brow. "Well, that's very Christian and all, but how am I supposed to drive back here when Grandma Tyler's car is in Maine?"

"You don't have to worry about that, Duff. That old farmhouse will be worth a mint to anyone who wants to run away from civilization and live among the moose in northern Maine—and, you'll have a brand new car. I'll have it shipped down here. You can drive that back."

"Are you going up to Maine?" he asked.

"Yes, I'll drive up tomorrow—I think there will just be a memorial service, not an actual funeral, and she wanted to be cremated, so no body. You can take your time coming up, as I have to deal with a lot of smaller stuff before we get to the document signings." She gave a slight laugh. "I can't even imagine what that house looks like."

He raised an eyebrow. "So I can stop and see some sights along the way, or spend a day or two in DC if I want to? Are you sure you don't need me?"

Her laugh had tinkled like music in the background, and all of a sudden he was glad to be going home. He had missed her and the picturesque town of Stockbridge where he had grown up.

In a good mood, anticipating the trip, as well as being out of the office for two weeks, he finished packing, closed the suitcase and snapped the lock. At first dismayed by the idea of driving fifteen hundred miles in his old car, he thought he might actually enjoy the trip.

And, he thought, there was the Tanya situation, business to be settled there.

Five

As he drove down Indiantown Road toward I-95, he decided suddenly to get a coffee from the Starbucks on the corner. But traffic was heavy, and he missed his chance to exit into the drive-around. He had no choice but to drive until he found a turnaround, and when he did, the light was red—it seemed forever—before he could continue.

He drove into the coffee shop's circular driveway just as Marisol's red car exited from the other side. He tooted his horn and waved, but the girls seemed not to notice him. Another identical red Focus pulled up behind them, further hindering his view. As he rounded the building, he found his way blocked by cars waiting in the drive-thru lane, and one very large moving van.

He had a sudden thought: he was glad they hadn't seen him. He didn't want them to think he would be following them. That would be stalking and that was something Raina would never forgive him for. No, she sure wouldn't, not with that strong mind and independent streak of hers.

From his position, he could see the entrance to 95, but not to the turnpike, an eighth of a mile beyond. He twisted around and craned his neck as far out the window as he could, watching for the red car. He saw it exit for the main road, and its twin suddenly pulled around and went out ahead of Marisol's car. Or—was it Marisol's car? Maybe she had gone ahead of the other vehicle. Confused, he watched them head west on Indiantown Road where both I-95 and Florida's Turnpike had entrances. He saw one car take I-95, and the other continued on, but he had lost track of which car was which. Well, he had to take one of those highways, and I-95 went directly north, which is where he wanted to go, so he opted for that one, assuming Raina and Marisol would head for Orlando and all the attractions there via the turnpike. Okay, good, that meant he would take I-95, which would be slower, but take him more directly north. At least he knew where to go to not be following them, once he got out of the Starbucks trap.

"I feel like freakin' Jim Carrey," he muttered, feeling amusement at himself as he waited for the cars to move through the drive-thru. "I'm getting everything messed up, and everything that could go wrong is going wrong." It took fifteen minutes before he was able to move through and get back on the road. He hit the ramp to I-95 and got on it smoothly. He half-expected the big semi behind him to lose its brakes and crash into him, or a fifteen-foot alligator to decide to cross the road at that particular moment and tie up all the traffic.

Duff wasn't in any hurry, and he enjoyed driving fast. It was a thing with him, and one that Raina repeated called him on. Once on the highway, where traffic was mercifully slight, he drove as fast as he dared, pretending he was already behind the wheel of the Lexus instead of the broken-down Toyota, keeping a keen eye out for cops.

"Yeah, I know you guys like to hide behind billboards or in one of those small strands of trees. I'm not speeding. I'm onto you." It was a beautiful day, his gas tank was full, he had thought to bring a cooler with water and soft drinks, and there were sandwiches packed for lunch in case he got hungry. The sky was that particular, beautiful azure blue that he'd only seen in Florida. He would not push himself, but make the trip in three days. If anything looked interesting along the way, he would stop and see it. He was grateful his mom had given him that option, and said not to hurry.

The straight, endless road lulled him. He turned on the car radio. He had a choice of a preacher predicting the end of the world and what he had to do to earn salvation, a conservative talk show host trying to persuade his dedicated audience that all Democrats were a pack of lying dogs, and a station whining out country music. The songs about deserting wives and dying dogs seemed to be the best choice, so he half- listened, singing along and complaining that it was a swell time for Lucille to leave him, with four crying children and a crop in the field. He wished he'd brought along some CDs of Mozart, or an opera or two. Well, he had been bound to forget something, so he was stuck with Lucille. With luck he'd find a place to buy some books on tape.

A cowboy on the radio lamented that someone he loved "didn't know him," and Duff began to sing along with him. He knew that song; he had thought more than once when he'd heard it on the oldies stations that Dianne sometimes had on at the office, that it was so true of him and Raina. He gave her his hand; she didn't know him. She said hello, but she didn't know him. He tried to show her how much he cared, but it was all in vain. She didn't know who he really was.

The next song that came on was one with which he was not familiar. It seemed to be about a man and woman in love, but she had a husband, who wasn't him, and he had a wife, who wasn't her. Each one wondered what the other was going to do about her husband, or what to do about his wife. Duff, caught up in the silly lyrics in spite of himself, laughed and sang along with the refrain as he listened.

He glanced at the car clock. Twelve-thirty. Nature was calling. He could take one of the upcoming exits, visit a gas station, find an attractive place to stop and eat his lunch in a bucolic setting. Lost in the absurdity of the song, he missed the second of a pair of upcoming exits, but noticed when the red car whizzed by him and took it.

He stretched his neck to stare after the car. "Is that Raina and Marisol? I thought they were taking the turnpike. When did they make the switch to 95?" Or, had he been mistaken that they had taken Florida's Turnpike? Maybe he had watched the wrong car, and made a fatal mistake, even while trying so hard to make sure he wasn't following them. Yeah, there are lots of red cars like Marisol's. Couldn't have been them. He shook his head. No telling when or why they had made the switch, or whether they had been on the Thruway all along. But better he had missed that exit. Much as he would love to join them for lunch somewhere, he couldn't risk Raina's thinking he was following her, even if it would be just to protect her. She'd made it abundantly clear she didn't want that…he shuddered. She might even interpret it as stalking. No way would he want her to think that. There had to be more than one restaurant off that exit. If he saw their car, he would keep going to the next fast food joint or gas station—he could manage that, but he didn't think he could last twenty minutes to the next exit.

Nature became insistent. "Maybe I can back up to the first exit. If there aren't any cops, I might get away with that. Well, nothing ventured, nothing gained." Pulling over to the grass on the side of the road, he threw the gearshift into reverse, and began to back up slowly. Vehicles passed him at what seemed super-fast speeds, since they were going one way and he the other. Nevertheless, he thought he had made it. He could see the exit in his rear-view mirror.

"Just a couple of hundred feet more. I'm going to make it." Then—a police car loomed in the distance. Duff stopped and threw the gear into first, and flicked on his turn signal, as if he had just stopped for a break. It was time for lunch after all. The cruiser passed him, slowed and pulled over into one of the breaks in the median. Then law could sit there, but a prominent No U Turn sign warned motorists not to cut through.

The cop car waited.

Duff waited. Damn it—I'm going to have to get out and take a leak by the side of the road if he doesn't move on. And that will be embarrassing right out here in the open. And I might just get a ticket for that anyway. The minutes crawled back. Finally, realizing that the officer intended to sit there until Duff made a move, he pulled away from the side of the road and edged into the traffic. The cruiser did the same, staying some distance behind Duff.

Frustrated, Duff banged on the steering wheel, yelling out loud. "What is it with you, guy? Do you have to ruin my day, not to mention my whole freakin' life, maybe?"

He passed a sign which announced: Next Exit 10 Miles."

"Great! Just great! It'll take me ten minutes to get there, five minutes to find a gas station, and by that time—"

Suddenly the police cruiser took off like a bat out of hell and flew past him, lights on, siren wailing.

Duff threw a longing look at the breaks in the median, where the No U Turn signs lurked like silent sentinels. Traffic had lessened, and he could see well in all directions. He seemed to be almost alone on the road, and for sure there were no billboards or copses of trees where cops could hide. Nature nudged insistently. He had to chance it, get back to the previous exit.

He slowed his speed, looked around one more time to be sure the law was nowhere to be seen, and with his heart beating hard, made the forbidden U turn and headed back in the other direction.

And there, materializing out of nowhere, was a cruiser, swooping down on him, blue lights flashing.

Resigned, his spirits sinking lower than a submarine, Duff pulled his vehicle over.

"License, registration, insurance." The cop was a burly black guy, and Duff's hopes sunk even more. He could probably expect no mercy. He looked like the type who would take all the info back to the cruiser, and sit there twenty minutes, making Duff wait. Well, that would prove interesting.

To his surprise, the officer checked Duff's information, handed it all back, and said, "You know you can't make a U turn there, don't you?"

"Yeah," Duff replied, in no mood for polite conversation.

"Why did you then? Why couldn't you wait for the next exit?"

"Because I need to find a gas station—right now." Duff said, staring at the steering wheel. "I missed the exit."

The cop peered at the gas gauge. You have half a tank left. You could easily make it to the next exit."

"That's not why I need the gas station." He sifted uncomfortably in his seat. "And I didn't really want to have to do that in public—"

Surprisingly, the cop laughed. He had a big smile and very white teeth.

"Well, I'm in a good mood today, so I'm going to let you go. But don't do it again."

Six

In a few minutes, Duff accessed the exit going south instead of north, but there was only one road, which wound along through fields with cows and horses, and orange groves. Central Florida—it was another world from the coastal areas. He pulled into the nearest gas station and took care of business. Jumping back in the car, he looked for a place where he could pull over, get out and walk a bit to loosen up his tight joints, and eat his lunch.

There were some people sitting under palm trees at one of several picnic tables in a meadow-like setting, near a fruit stand which seemed to be operated by people who lived in a nearby, small stucco house. Other visitors poked around among the fruit and vegetable stands.

Duff looked around, considering. He could join the group and sit at one of the tables, or look for a place where he could sit alone and worry about Raina in private.

A barbed wire fence ran behind the picnic tables, cutting them off from the orchard, which stretched from the side of the road to the north and east. Beyond that there seemed to be a meadow with a few brown cows, peacefully grazing.

"How now, brown cow. You're going to have company." He edged the car down the road, where a slight curve still hugged the meadow, but hid the fruit stand. Pulling the car over into the long grass at the side of the road, he let out a long sigh of relief.

"Well," he said, "I'll just have a picnic, too." He got out and grabbed a blanket from the back seat. He carried the small cooler and the remainder of his lunch, climbed over the barbed wire fence, which wasn't too much of a feat with his long legs, and ventured into the orchard. Although the fruit stand was just beyond a strand of trees, he would not be particularly noticed if he settled down there. He glanced toward the cows. They raised their heads and regarded him for a long moment before returning to their grazing, but didn't seem to object to his sharing their space.

The trees provided a welcome leafy canopy. Duff spread a blanket on the grass and sank down on it, glad to be out from behind the wheel. It felt so good to relax. Florida-hot, but he felt comfortable, shaded by the trees. He missed New England, and hoped to go back there someday, but he'd gotten used to Florida, and appreciated the state for what it was. He'd come here after earning his master's degree, then finding himself out of money and in debt, decided to get a job, doing anything—well, almost anything while he sent out letters and his resumè to colleges all over the East.

"Yeah," he said out loud. "Got a job at Northlake Industries and met my future wife. She just doesn't know it yet."

He leaned back against one of the large trees, feeling as comfortable as if it were a Barcalounger, daydreaming about the life he and Raina would have together. No, she didn't think so now, but Duff felt no doubt at all about the fact that he would spend his life with that particular woman. He knew it in his bones. He pictured her pretty face in his mind. He heard her tinkling laughter...he sat up with a jerk. That was her tinkling laughter, for sure! He peered around the tree, searching among the people at the picnic tables. Yes, there they were—Raina and Marisol. How had he not seen them before—how had he missed their car? Then, stretching a bit more, he saw the rear bumper of Marisol's car, parked on the opposite side of the farm stand. He wouldn't have seen it from the exit road.

They must have arrived after him, and since his car was around the swoop in the road, they hadn't seen it.

He considered going over and spending a few minutes with them. They were at the same place accidentally, after all. His being there at the same time wasn't at all intentional. In fact, he had tried not to be in the same place at the same time. But as he thought about it, he knew that Raina would not be glad to see him. She wanted this time alone with Marisol. She wanted a vacation from his love. He sighed, as he turned away. Raina, you're drivin' me crazy! Literally. He almost laughed. This trip wasn't starting off very well. He had already wasted half an hour going absolutely nowhere. Fate pulled some dirty tricks sometimes.

He'd better get out of there before they saw him. He jumped to his feet, threw everything into the cooler, grabbed the blanket, and began to race through the trees. He reached the open area where the trees ended, and ran toward the truck, the cooler knocking him in the legs as he ran.

He heard the bull before he saw it. He hadn't noticed the tear in the barbed wire fence, which kept the cattle out of the orchard. He glanced behind him and his heart felt as though it had fallen into a bucket of thistles. A big, black bull was charging, with its head lowered, through the opening straight toward him.

Duff wasn't conscious of making any noise, but he did hear someone yelling in fright. He didn't realize he was capable of making such a primitive sound. He dropped the cooler, then made the biggest mistake he could have made. He held up the blanket in front of him and waved it, as if trying to hide himself behind it and divert the bull's attention. It bellowed and charged right for him. Duff ran for the fence, ran for his life. He hoped the trees and the distance shielded him from the fruit stand's view.

When he reached it, his long legs refused to carry him over it with the ease he had crossed it before. He fell on the barbed wire, feeling it pierce his skin, but he had no choice. He heard the bull close in behind him, snorting in fury. Duff rolled over the fence to safety, hearing his clothing tear. He didn't care. He jumped into his car and slammed the door. The bull stopped on the other side of the fence and glared at him, pawing the ground with one hoof.

Duff slumped back against the seat. He examined a couple of places on his arms which were bleeding, but not that badly. It was his clothing which had taken the brunt of the abuse. Obviously, he would have to find a place to change before he could check into a motel.

He shook his fist at the bull, who showed no sign of retreat. "If I had wanted to be a toreador, I would have been born in Spain!"

He had to slide over into the driver's seat, since he had jumped into the passenger's side of the vehicle. He put the key in the ignition and started it up. Pulling out onto the road, he suddenly doubled over, laughing. What a story he would have to tell someday, but probably nobody would believe him.

Seven

"Oh, I've heard so much about this place!" Raina could hardly sit still as they drove into the palm tree-lined driveway of the Nickelodean complex. The many-storied resort hotel sported colorful triangle-shaped additions on the roof, and cartoon characters grinned from the round spaces in them.

Marisol nodded. "I think it's better for people with kids, and not twentyishers like us, but I'm willing to give it a try."

"It looks like such fun just being here. I'm so glad we got off ninety-five and headed over here. The swim-with-dolphins thing sounds amazing, and we can always cut back to St. Augustine after we do this." Raina wriggled in her seat as she looked around, trying to see everything. "It's just that I've wanted to come here ever since I was a kid, and a lot of my friends had been here and that's all they could talk about, but my folks pooh-poohed the whole thing. They couldn't have afforded it anyway, so this is a dream come true for me, even if I do have to pay for it myself. And—" she added, with a defiant glance at Marisol, "I want to get slimed with that green stuff they spray over everyone."

Marisol laughed and rolled her eyes. "Suit yourself. I'll skip that one."

They settled into their rooms. They had been given a suite with two bedrooms and a tiny kitchen area with a refrigerator, stove top and microwave.

"We should have brought some food," Marisol said. "We could have cooked for ourselves and saved some money. Plus we could have eaten better," she added. "All they have here are fast-food places." She wrinkled her nose. "I'm gonna miss Mama's home cooking."

Raina laughed. "I'm not. I'm addicted to McDonald's and Kentucky Fried." She flopped on the full-sized bed, stretched out and sighed. "Ah, I'm in heaven."

Marisol placed the bottles of white wine she had bought for herself, and the beer that Raina preferred into the refrigerator. "You know, if you ever get serious with Duff, you're going to have to learn to cook decent food. I have a feeling he's not a fast-food guy."

"I know he's not, but who says I'm ever going to get serious with him?" Raina stretched again, loving the feel of her muscles loosening after the cramped hours in the car. "I keep telling you, and him, that I'm just not his type." She flopped over on her side and gazed at Marisol. "I don't know what he sees in me, honestly, I don't."

Marisol walked over and sat on the edge of the bed. "He's in love with you, Raina. Love isn't always logical. Look at *Pretty Woman.* Should a successful businessman fall in love with a prostitute?"

Raina sat bolt upright, offended to the core. "Marisol! I'm not a prostitute!"

Marisol inclined her head to one side. "Of course not. I didn't say that, or mean that."

"What did you mean, then?"

"I just meant that people who are really far apart in some areas—financial, social, educational, whatever—often fall in love and are perfectly suited to each other, in spite of what everyone else thinks." She winked at Raina. "Sometimes even in spite of what they themselves think."

Raina felt a flare of irritation. "So you think I'm inferior to Duff? Why are you my friend if I'm such a loser?"

"I didn't say that either!" Marisol yelled. "I'm not getting across what I mean."

"Well, what do you mean?" Hands on her hips, she scowled at her best friend.

"I mean I think you could be a good match for Duff—in spite of the differences in education and interests that you keep stressing. You're pretty—he obviously likes that, you are smart and capable, even if it's not in the same way he is, and in time you might come to like all these cultural things he's so crazy about."

"So now you're a match-maker?" Raina teased, not trying to eliminate the trace of sarcasm that leaked through.

Marisol grinned at her. "Well, I did pretty well with Andrea and Greg, didn't I? Fixed them up on a blind date and a year later they got married."

Raina shrugged. "Well, that was lucky for them, but…"

"And my brother, Juan. Pushed him to ask Sophia out when he thought she would never go out with him, and now they're talking wedding bells and honeymoons."

Raina pouted. "But he'll never learn to appreciate the things I enjoy—Friday nights at the neighborhood bar, Jim Carrey movies, the circus…" She shrugged. "Beer and a fish fry. I can't even identify what the food is at the restaurants he takes me to."

"But you could…now, don't take this wrong, Raina, but I think you're meant for better things than the life you're living now. You could elevate yourself, be everything you're meant to be, and a marriage to someone like Duff is the ticket. He has the passport to a better life."

Raina didn't say anything for a few minutes, while she pondered what Marisol had said. What was wrong with the way she was now? She'd never had aspirations for anything more than her parents had, what they'd prepared her for. Her father worked at the local factory, her mother was an LPN and made decent money. She and Luis had never gone to college, although she had taken a summer business course. They were pleased with the job she had now. Why did she need to be 'better'?

A sudden thought occurred to her. "Mare, do you think Duff would actually follow us on this trip?"

Marisol furled her brow. "Why on earth would he do that?"

"Well, he was very upset about our going on a road trip by ourselves. And he's so protective." She jumped off the bed, went over to the window and looked out. "I wouldn't be surprised if he tailed us every step of the way."

Marisol shook her head and laughed. "Oh, Raina, even Duff wouldn't stoop to that. That's stalking. He'd never do that. Besides, his grandmother died, remember? He'd fly up north, not drive all that way."

"I guess you're right." Raina sank into one of the chairs by the window. "But—how do we know he didn't just make all that up about his grandmother dying so he could drive along and keep an eye on me?"

"I just don't think he'd do that. He's a decent guy. Ethical. Let's go to the pool."

"I hope you're right. Because if I get just one glimpse of Michael Duffy on this trip, I will never speak to him again. Ever." She began to rifle through her suitcase. She held up two bikinis. "Which do you like better, the pink or the black?"

Marisol sighed. "Raina..."

Raina threw the black suit on the bed and headed toward the bathroom carrying the pink one. "I don't want to talk about it anymore. Let's go to the pool and view the scenery."

"Who will all be young moms who have a ring on the third finger and little kids in tow," Marisol yelled after her, just before the door closed.

Eight

Back on the road, Duff noticed the sign indicating the exit that would take him to Florida's Turnpike, the alternate north-south route through the state. On impulse, he took it. *If Raina and Marisol on are 95, I'd better be on another road. This will slow me down a bit, but I'll drive a couple hours longer than I ordinarily would to make up the time. I just don't want them to think I'm following them—especially since I told them I was flying up. She gets one glance at me, I'm in big trouble. Finished. Blotto.*

Nearing Orlando, he thought about his one trip to Disneyworld when he was nine or ten years old. Grandma Victoria Gray had suggested and financed the trip shortly after his father had died. That was Granny. Replace the sorrow with something pleasant, and maybe the pain wouldn't be so bad. But Duff had never liked cartoons, didn't find anything funny in the funny papers, and Disney had been a let-down for him. He felt like he'd been dropped into the middle of one of those slapstick bunny-hits-beaver-who-yanks beaver's-tail-who—

Pop! The Toyota swerved, and Duff knew immediately what had happened. He braked carefully, flicked on his directional and pulled over to the side of the road. The gravel grated and squeaked under his wheels.

He hopped out of the car, and checked his tires, knowing what he was going to find. The back right tire was flat as a pancake.

There was nothing for it but to change the tire to the mini-spare. Sure, he grimaced as he struggled with the tire... he might be an intellectual but he wasn't entirely helpless mechanically. He could change a tire. He stood and rubbed the grime off his already torn and filthy clothing. As soon as that chore was done, he drove until the next exit and a sign directed him to a Texaco station. Luckily, they did have a repair shop.

The scruffy young garage mechanic looked him up and down. "What the hell happened to you?"

Duff sighed. "You wouldn't believe it if I told you. Not even three hours on the road and I get a flat tire," he complained as the mechanic straightened up from looking at the left front wheel.

"By the sounds of this car, you got a lot more trouble than just the tire," Ernie replied, brushing his oily black hair out of his eyes. "Heard it when you drove in. You'd best find a place to stay while we look it over."

Duff's spirits sank. "How do I get there without a car?"

"You find a place, we'll getcha over there."

Duff knew he had no choice. He couldn't take a chance on the car breaking down on a fifteen-hundred-mile drive. He checked for motels on his iPhone, and found to his amazement that there was nothing available. Except at a shabby, run-down place called the Blue Vision, which he remembered passing a mile or so back, where someone said they had a room, just one room, and if he wanted it, he'd better hurry, as they were expecting a convention in town. Or—the Nickelodean, which would cost him plenty for even a single room for one night.

He grinned and booked a room. He remembered the place; he'd been there as a child, on the Disney visit, and had fond memories of it. Though he hadn't taken to the cartoon-world, the whole experience had morphed into a fuzzy but pleasant snapshot of his childhood, the good memories of when he had been there with his mother and Grandma Victoria. Why not let his inner child come out to play, and treat himself to one last glimpse of that childhood memory?

He tucked the phone in his pocket. "Nickolodean," He told Ernie.

Ernie's eyebrows shot upward, but he gestured to another attendant, garbed as Ernie was in navy blue coveralls with 'Ted' scrawled in red thread above his chest pocket.

"Nickelodean," he instructed Ted. He handed Duff a business card. "Call me tomorrow, early as you want to. I'll have a diagnosis for you by then and an estimate."

"Which means I'll have to spend two nights here?"

Ernie shrugged. "Depends on what I find. Call me, I'll letcha know."

Ted seemed to be the silent type, as he didn't have much to say, and Duff wasn't much in the mood for casual conversation either. He swung his long legs into the passenger seat of the black truck. Within a few minutes, they drove onto the winding road that circled the huge building. Ted stopped at the office entrance, got out and unloaded Duff's suitcase.

"Call us in the morning about the car," he muttered, and without another glance at Duff, jumped back into the car. Duff turned to go into the office, and at just that moment a red car sped past him on the left and headed into the parking lot. It would have to be an incredible coincidence if it turned out to be Marisol's car. Instinctively, he ducked down, hoping the garage's truck had hidden him.

Marisol's car, oh no, it can't be! But it is. He knew her car, every scratch, every dent, and he recognized backs of their heads as they passed by.

Obviously they hadn't seen him. Ted began to drive away, and Duff chased him, pounding on the front fender and yelling, "Stop! Stop! I can't stay here!"

Ted rolled down the window. "What?"

Duff pulled on the passenger side door handle. Locked. "Let me in, I can't stay here."

"Why the hell not?"

Duff pounded on the window. "Open the door, Ted. Take me to the Blue Vision." He crouched down as he watched Marisol park the car, and the two girls get out. "Ted, open the goddam door!"

When Ted clicked the door open, Duff tossed his suitcase into the back and jumped into the vehicle. "The Blue Vision," he gasped. Ted threw him an incredulous glance, muttered something, and started the car up again. Duff sank as low as he could in the seat and buried his head in his arms as Ted circled the parking lot, passing Raina and Marisol just as they emerged from their car.

Ted drove into the parking lot of the Blue Vision, and Duff asked him to wait while he ran into the office, hoping that one room was still there. The place wasn't much, but he had to have a place to spend the night. There was a hamburger joint across the street. He could buy some hopefully not too greasy a dinner and take it into his room. He'd open the bottle of expensive French wine he'd tucked into his suitcase and pay for a foreign film on the TV. He assumed even a motel as shabby as this would have a working TV. He loved movies with subtitles. That way, he got the gist of the movie, got the real flavor of the culture through the sound of the language, even if he couldn't understand it all. It made him feel as if he were really there, experiencing the country and the people in person. Not just watching something Hollywood had thrown together.

The only time he'd taken Raina to a foreign film with subtitles she'd fallen asleep.

Nine

To the side of the low pink building, flanked by scraggly trees, Duff saw a small pool. A middle-aged couple sat at one of the white, wrought iron tables. And a scrawny, long-haired girl in a yellow bikini perched on the side, dangling her feet in the water. Well, at least he could get wet, maybe soak away some of the day's frustrations.

He swung open the creaking door which looked as if it were hanging on to its hinges with pure will power, and went into the motel office.

"One night?" the bored young clerk, tired-eyed and stringy-haired, asked. Her name tag said 'Candee.'

"Yes," Duff said.

"Do you think you might be staying longer?"

"No. I'm driving up north. Just staying overnight. Well, possibly two, but I hope not."

"You hope not? Do you want to stay here or not?"

"Well, yes, but you see my car is being repaired, and as soon as I can leave, I need to get back on the road."

"We have a convention coming in Thursday. They might take up all the rooms if you don't have yours already reserved."

"Don't they already have their rooms reserved?"

She shrugged. "All I know is what I'm told. I can't guarantee you a room after tonight if you don't reserve in advance."

He shook his head, and presented her with his Visa card. "One night, Candee—" he pronounced it with a hard 'C' and she cut him off.

"It's pronounced like Sandie, with an 'S'."

"Then why is it spelled with a 'C'?"

She looked at him in exasperation. "My twin is Cindee with a soft 'C'. My mother wanted another C name with a soft 'C' sound."

A roly-poly woman with the same stringy red hair popped out of the inner office. "Problem here, Candee?" She said it like 'Sandy.'

"Mister—" she glanced at his Visa card. "Mr. Duffy doesn't know whether he's staying one night or more. I told him he had to reserve in advance to be sure of having the room after tonight."

Mrs. Roly Poly set her hands on her hips and glared at him. "Why are you giving my daughter a hard time, Mr. Duffy? Do you want the room or not?"

He slid the card over to Candee. "I do, but only one night, please."

Candee's mom continued to stare at him. "We have a convention coming in Thursday night. We can't guarantee you a room unless you book for three nights."

"Thank you, but I will only be here for one night."

Candee processed the information and he signed the registration sheet, with her mom standing there, looking on with a disapproving expression.

Candee handed Duff the room key. Without looking at him, she waved her hand toward the end of the room where there was a counter with a coffee pot, and several tables and chairs. "Our special Southern breakfast with grits, sausage and white gravy is served from six until ten. Will you be having breakfast with us?"

He snatched the key and turned toward the door. "I'll play it by eye."

She eyed him suspiciously. "By eye? What do you mean by that?"

"Oh, I forgot, by ear, yes. It's just something I say."

He turned to leave the office. He heard Candee say to her mom,

"He's weird." Not the first time he'd been called that, and he had no aspirations to date Candee so it really didn't matter.

As he left the office, he met two women going in. "Do they still have some rooms?" asked one of them. "The King Palm Motel down the road is all filled up."

Duff shrugged and shook his head. "Danged if I know. Good luck."

The woman raised her eyebrows as he held the door open for her and her companion.

"And," he added, "it's pronounced Sandee, as with an 'S', and not Candee with a 'C'."

He looked around for Ted, but the truck had gone. He headed for his room.

Ten

He put on his swim trunks and headed for the pool, taking his cell phone with him.

The young couple who had been there before he checked in was still there. He waded into the pool and sat on the lowest step, relishing the feel of the warm water on his skin. He pressed her number.

He couldn't wait to hear Raina's voice. When she answered, it sent shivers all through him.

"Duff! It's vacation. You're not supposed to call me. I've only been gone one day. How can I feel like I'm on vacation, and it's partly you I'm on vacation from."

"Oh, Raina," he said, hearing the longing in his own voice, "this is drivin' me crazy. I need you like the bumblebee needs honey. More than fame, more than money."

She sighed. "Is that from some poem I'm supposed to recognize? Robert Frost, maybe?"

He laughed. "No, I just made it up. Where are you?"

"In Orlando at the Nickelodean. Where are you?"

He almost blurted out—"Just down the street from the Nickelodean," but caught himself in time. She couldn't know he was so close and that he had seen them. In fact, if she thought he was anywhere near them, she would think he was following them, and nothing he could say would hold any water with her. It would be the end of his hopes, period. He had to make her think he was—in Maine. That's it; he was in Maine.

"Maine," he fibbed, crossing his fingers. "I flew up today and got here about two o'clock." He made his voice mournful. "Mom is just devastated. She and Granny were so close, and this was so sudden."

She actually sounded sympathetic. "I'm so sorry, Duff. I hope it hasn't made your mom's condition worse."

"Oh, no, she's fine," he said breezily, before he realized he'd told them all that she had a health problem. "Uhm...her condition seems to be on hold right now."

"What exactly is her condition?" Raina asked.

"Nerves," he improvised. "Some days she's okay, others not so good."

"Hmm," Raina murmured, not sounding convinced.

He attempted to change the subject. "I bet you're out there lying in the sun, right? Brr...I sure miss the Florida sunshine."

The young woman lowered her book, and stared at him.

"But it's July," Raina protested. "Even Maine is warm in July, isn't it?"

Another gaffe. This fibbing business sure wasn't easy. "Well, usually," he said. "But it's gray and rainy today, and only about sixty degrees. We even have a fire in the fireplace." He made himself shiver. "Brrr."

The woman on the chaise looked up at the sky and back at Duff. She picked up a glass from the pavement, poured some wine into it from the bottle, and sipped it, still regarding Duff with a puzzled expression.

"Well, at least your mom won't have to worry about cooking," Raina's voice said on the other end of the line. "That's one good thing."

Puzzled, he asked, "Why not?"

She paused. "Duff, are the traditions that different in Maine? Every time we had a friend or relative die, everyone brought casseroles and other kinds of food. That's what they do when someone dies."

"Oh, oh sure," he said lamely. "I saw some ladies come in. We have coq au vin, moussaka, a couple of quiches…" He trailed off as the silence on the other end weighed more than any words she might say.

"Duff, I seriously doubt the ladies of rural Maine ever even heard of moussaka, let alone whip it up for a sympathy casserole. Now, if you said mouse pie, I might be convinced."

"Yeah, maybe," he said. "I didn't look that closely. Eggplant something, or maybe it was beets. Look, Raina, I just wanted to call and see how you are doing. Going to Disney tomorrow?"

"Hmmmmm, I don't know," she said. "Marisol wants to go to that swim-with-the-dolphins thing, so I guess we'll do that."

"Well, have a blast. Just a sec, Raina." He put his hand lightly over the phone and made his voice higher. Michael! Michael! Where are you? "Mom's calling me, Raina, I have to go now. But I'll check in with you tomorrow. Bye!"

The woman with the book made a choking sound. He flashed her a glance and shrugged his shoulders. "Ya gotta do whatcha gotta do."

With a feeling of satisfaction, he skidded the phone across the concrete toward his shoes under one of the chairs. He let himself slip into the water, and lay there, basking in the Florida sun, and feeling only a little guilty with the fabrications he had spun. He was a little disappointed about the swim-with-dolphins thing, because if his car wasn't ready tomorrow, he'd have liked to have done that. Now he'd have to find some other way to pass the time. Maybe, with luck, the car would be ready.

Duff grinned. Tomorrow he would have to tell Raina about Andrew Wyeth, who'd had a summer home in Maine.

Eleven

Raina clicked off her phone, but her conversation with Duff left her puzzled. Marisol turned over in her chaise and looked at her. "How're things in Maine?"

"Danged if I know. His whole family must be about as weird as he is. That's just another reason why I shouldn't get further involved with him"

Marisol reached for her sun lotion. "Oh, yeah? What did he say?"

She told Marisol the gist of their conversation, including the temperature and the kind of casseroles the natives had brought the grieving family.

Marisol laughed. "That's not impossible, you know."

"Not impossible, but improbable. And how about it's being sixty degrees there? I saw the national weather report this morning, and New England is supposed to be having a heat wave."

"Maybe he said eighty, not sixty."

"He sounded as though he was shivering."

Marisol shrugged and shook her head.

"Ya'know," Raina said, looking thoughtfully into the distance. "He could be following us, in some motel just down the street, and pretending to be in Maine. Do you think he'd do that, Mar?"

Marisol put her hand on Raina's arm. "No. No, I really don't. He wouldn't do that. He has respect for your privacy. He's one of the good guys, Raina."

Raina bit her lip. "Hmm. And he does know I would have nothing more to do with him ever, if he were following us and we caught him."

"That he does," agreed Marisol. "Now let stop worrying about that." She held up the tube of sunscreen. "Want me to do your back?"

Raina grinned at her. "You always have my back, don't you?"

~ * ~

In the morning, Duff watched the local and national news in bed, after making himself a cup of Hawaiian Kona coffee with the coffee and the pot he had brought with him. He showered and dressed, hoping the motel breakfast would be good. Well, decent. Edible.

Candee's mother held down the fort at the front desk, and gave him a granite smile as he came in. "Breakfast on the house. Help yourself." He turned to thank her, but noticed she was longer looking at him.

"Thanks," he muttered to no one in particular.

A row of steel serving pans with covers lined the counter. He picked up a plate and opened the first one. Limp bacon swimming in its own grease. No thanks. He replaced the cover. The next serving dish held scrambled eggs—much too runny for his taste. He moved on.

"The sausage, biscuits and gravy are the best in the state," Mrs. Roly Poly called from across the room. "My sister has a catering service, and she provides 'em for us. Fresh every day. Don't pass them up."

Afraid of what he would find, he uncovered the next dish, which was partitioned, with biscuits in one side, and thin, lumpy white gravy on the other. With the other hand he opened the last server. That held the sausage, which looked as unappetizing as the bacon.

"Jest help yerself," Candee's mother called. "Don't be shy."

He felt trapped. He didn't want to eat anything he'd seen, but he didn't want to offend Mrs. Roly Poly either. He took a breath, put two biscuits on his plate, and ladled gravy over it. It looked revolting. He added one of the huge pink sausages. He grimaced. You wouldn't have any trouble believing it was once a pig.

He put the plate on one of the tables and went back for orange juice. As he returned to his table and took a seat, he glanced over at Candee's mom. She laid a beatific smile on him, and folded her hands on the counter, as she waited to see his reaction to his first bite.

He took a bite, swallowed, and waved his fork at her. "Wonderful!"

He forced down bite after bite of the awful stuff, trying not to wretch, and she stood there, smiling and watching him with obvious pleasure. When he came to the sausage, his stomach nearly revolted. It was so big...so fleshy...so pink...so reminiscent of something else. He didn't even want to think about that comparison as he choked it down.

Finally finished, he waved his napkin at Candee's mom. "Wow! That was something, that was really something!"

She came out from behind the desk and waddled across the room faster than he would have given her credit for being able to do. Before he realized what she was doing, she had filled another plate with biscuits, poured the gravy over it, and added two more of the revolting sausages.

"Oh, no—I couldn't—" he began, but she plunked the plate down in front of him. "Jest knew you'd love that. Now, you're a good-sized boy, and you need a hearty breakfast before you go do whatever yer gonna do today, so chow down, boy."

His stomach already protesting, Duff stared up at her, and wished he'd had the sense to go to McDonald's.

Twelve

Duff would have preferred to experience a swim with the dolphins, but since Raina and Marisol were headed there, he didn't dare. He was five minutes from Disneyworld, so he might as well spend the day there. For sure he couldn't sit around the Blue Vision, and it seemed a shame to spend the sunny day reading, even if he had anything worth reading. So Disney it was.

Duff grinned as he thought how Granny Gray would laugh when he told her he'd been back to Magic Kingdom, which hadn't particularly thrilled him even when he was young. But he would look at it all differently now that he recognized Walt Disney's incredible talent. After all, cartooning was a form of art, even if he didn't much appreciate it. He'd just been a different sort of kid, one who'd rather wander around a museum or art gallery or sit for hours lost in a book, than be a Boy Scout or play Little League baseball.

He'd done a stint in Scouts, but it never made much sense to him—working for badges in subjects he didn't care anything about. After two or three months of that, he discovered a small museum of natural history across from the Baptist Church where the Scouts met. His parents dropped him off, he went inside the church and waited until he saw them drive off, then crossed the street to the museum.

Every day when he supposedly went to Scouts, he spent the two hours in the museum, until he knew it by heart, and it was still interesting to him. If anyone worked there, he never saw them, and they didn't bother him. One day he went up a flight of stairs to see what was up there—after all, no one was telling him 'no.'

To his astonishment, the second floor was filled with marble statues, dozens of naked people standing or sitting around the room. It wasn't an exhibit; the room was probably used for storage. Spellbound, he toured the room, eventually daring to reach out and stroke an arm, a leg, a back. It was his introduction to classical sculpture, and the beginning of his intense interest in and love of art.

After a few visits, he felt as though he knew the various sculptures. They became friends, not so different from the people who attended the cocktail parties his parents occasionally gave. So he gave them names, walked around to room, pretending to be the host.

"Mrs. Harris, may I refill your wine glass for you?"

"Mr. Thompson, how is business lately?"

"Angela, have you met Scott Williams?"

In time his parents found out he hadn't attended Scouts in some time, so that was also the end of his ritual museum visits, but he still went there sometimes. It was a small town, and he had a lot of freedom to explore.

But, perhaps he hadn't given Disney a fair chance. At any rate, here he was, and yes, his car needed more work, and he with nothing to do. Might as well look at Disney from a newer perspective, and with any luck, perhaps he could entice the child still hiding inside to come out and play.

Duff called a taxi, waved a not-so-fond goodbye at Candee as he passed the registration desk, bought his ticket at the gate, and hopped on the steamship taking visitors across the pond to Magic Kingdom. He wandered aimlessly for a while, trying to see the park with fresh eyes, no prejudices against cartoon characters. He was impressed with how clean and well-kept it was.

He bought a three-foot tall stuffed Sleeping Beauty doll as a souvenir for Raina, before wondering in a panic how he would explain that to her, and wandered around with it under his arm. Duff knew that four or five rides were all one was likely to experience in a day's visit, what with the crowds and the standing in line. He paused when he reached the Peter Pan sky ride, and remembered he had rather enjoyed that one, probably because he'd seen *Peter Pan* on stage and loved the play.

He cast a quick look around, searching for Raina and Marisol, just in case. Nope, no trace of them. He got in the back of the line, feeling a little foolish, but also carefree and young again, and within twenty minutes he had boarded the little train.

A large young couple, both tall and overweight, struggled into the car ahead of him. "Too damn bad about Dolphin Kingdom," the woman said. "Closed for the only day we're gonna be here." She had long, bleached-blond hair that hung down her back, and when she shook her head, the strands nearly struck Duff in the face.

"Yep, woulda been a blast," the guy with her said, patting his huge stomach.

Yeah, they'd probably think you were one of them. Duff immediately felt guilty for his uncharitable thought—but he had to admit, the resemblance was there.

So the dolphins weren't having visitors today. Just his lousy luck. Now the chances were pretty darn good that Marisol and Raina were here at Magic Kingdom He had often heard Raina say how much she wanted to go there.

Dodging the woman's stringy hair, Duff managed to peer around the couple in front of him, and his breath caught as his whole body reacted in shock Yes, he certainly did recognize two familiar heads. Raina and Marisol—way down in one of the cars up front. They must have boarded before he got in line. He couldn't believe his bad luck. Why this ride, in all of the park, why this park of all of the places they could have gone—why this one?

He shrank down in his seat, although knowing they wouldn't spot him behind the obese couple, at least until they all disembarked.

It started off slowly, passing by scenes from the Peter Pan story, impeccably staged and lighted. The car swooped up high, slid down low, ran along the rails. Duff would have actually enjoyed himself had his heart not been beating with such anxiety about being seen. He clutched Sleeping Beauty to him, and endured the ride, until finally the cars began to stop and let passengers off.

He spotted Raina and Marisol as they staggered off the train, laughing and gripping each other's arms. He shrunk down in his seat, but they walked off, never glancing back.

Only two or three cars to go. He got ready to debark—but suddenly the train started up again, throwing him back in his sea. A weird creak, like steel grating against steel, sounded. Passengers looked at each other, confused. The train speeded up—faster than its usual route.

Duff listened as more strange noises echoed around the cavern. There were scraping noises, clanging sounds, a clatter like heavy pieces hitting each other. The train kept going, once around the tour, then again and again.

Was it even remotely possible for one of these rides to get stuck—but stuck as in not stopping, not as in not going?

At first the passengers laughed among themselves, making jokes about getting six rides for their money, and thoroughly enjoying themselves. But as the ride went around and around, with no hint that it would ever stop, the laughter and chatter gradually edged off. Kids began to cry, then scream in protest.

Duff, too, felt a jolt of concern. These things were all governed by computer programs, right?—and it was quite possible for a computer to run amok. There was nothing to do, however, but sit tight and try to endure the ride. Over and over again.

A man's tremulous voice came over a loudspeaker.

"Ladies, gentlemen, and kids: we regret that the Peter Pan adventure seems to have developed a glitch, and we have not been able to stop the train. We have our engineers and computer people working on it, and you need not worry about your safety. All we can say is we're sorry for this problem and you all will receive a free day's pass to the Magic Kingdom. Please be patient, and we'll keep you posted."

A dizzying two hours later, the train bumped to a halt, and Duff and the others staggered woozily off. Many of the children had been crying for nearly the whole time; others had fallen asleep. A few had vomited, and the cavern smelled like it. Others had needed a bathroom, and since none was available, they did what they needed to do if they had to. The stench was indescribable.

Duff unfolded himself from the seat and wobbled into the open, trailing Sleeping Beauty by one arm as if she were an uncooperative child, merging into the crowd of the curious who had gathered in front of the building. His head felt as if were stuffed with cotton and revolving on his neck, and his stomach lurched from his heavy, unwelcome breakfast. He headed for the parking lot as fast as he could go. All he wanted in the world was his lumpy bed in the seedy Blue Vision.

He didn't know when he'd feel well enough to give Raina a call.

Thirteen

The taxi let him off and Duff and staggered toward the Blue Vision's entrance.

On the way, he passed the pool. The young couple was there again, sitting in the same lounge chairs as before. Duff had a brain flash. They might as well be a couple of Duane Hanson's realistic people sculptures. Maybe they were. No, his common sense told him. *Sculptures don't move, and yesterday she had a drink and gave me some funny looks.*

The woman waved at him. "How's the weather in Maine?"

Yeah, maybe Hanson has figured out a way to computer-program them to act and react. The dinosaurs at Yale Museum of Natural History bellow and move...

She obviously expected an answer. "Still cold," he said with a limp wave in her direction.

"Coming out to the pool?"

"Not today, maybe tomorrow."

He made it to his room, although the key card failed to work the first three or four times he inserted it, but finally the green light flashed. He opened the door and fell on the bed, groaning. *I'm living*

Jim Carrey's movie life, he thought. *Everything I do gets a glitch in it. It would be funny if it weren't happening to me.*

Although physically drained, his brain refused to turn off the repetition of the Peter Pan ride. Around and around he went, until with a huge effort, he roused himself enough to call out for a pizza to be delivered to his room. The food helped, and a couple glasses of wine relaxed him further. He flicked on the television and watched whatever inane programs flashed before his eyes until fatigue finally took over.

~ * ~

He didn't awake until after ten the next morning.

"Oh, damn!" he said. "Breakfast is over. I missed the biscuits and gravy."

Cautiously, he stretched his arms and legs and found that everything worked, if a bit stiffly from being cramped in the Peter Pan train car for so long. His head felt better, too. He sat up, and yawned.

His next action, even before he showered, had to be to call Raina, and find out about her plans for the day.

She picked up right away. "I thought you'd call last night. I have something funny to tell you."

"I'm sorry," he improvised. "We had a wake last night, and many people came. Didn't get home until late, and then my mom was so upset..."

"Oh, never apologize for that!" Her voice dropped and became sympathetic. "I'm so thoughtless not to have asked. When will the funeral be?"

"What funeral?" he asked, his mind so busy picturing Raina as someone Renoir might have painted, all soft and white and feminine, her honey-colored hair licked by the French sun—

"Your grandmother's, of course! When is it scheduled?"

His brain whirled. What was today? Tuesday? Did they have funerals during the week? Or did they wait until the weekend? "Uhm, Thursday at two pm," he said, making his voice as sober as hers.

"What church?"

He clapped a hand over his forehead. His family wasn't connected with any church, but Grandma Victoria had often taken him with her... what was that big white church on the main street in Stockbridge? Oh, yeah. "Congregational," he said. "Tell me about the funny thing that happened. I'm so worn out with all the funeral talk around here."

"In a minute. That's not important now." She persisted with her questioning. "Who's the minister, or do Congregational churches have rectors or pastors or priests, or what?"

He didn't remember what they called the guy in the black robe with the white turned-around collar. He took a stab at it. "Priests. It's Father Joseph. We've met with him several times. Great guy. Tell me the funny story. I could use a laugh."

"Duff, don't get testy. You always tell me I never ask anything about your family, or where you grew up, and what your life was like. I'm just trying to be sympathetic to your loss."

"What loss?" He caught himself. "Oh, yes, that loss."

"Your grandmother, Duff."

"Yes, yes, of course. I'm just so tired of thinking about all that. It's tiring, y'know. I'd rather hear about something funny."

"You've only been there a day and a half, and already you're tired of hearing about it? I guess you weren't very close to her, were you? But you have to be there for your mom, Duff."

"Of course." He started to feel a headache coming on. "I have to go in a few minutes—tell me the funny story, and what your plans are for the day. I don't want to bring you down by dwelling on all the gloom around here."

She sighed. "Okay." She plunged into the account of what had happened to the Peter Pan ride, breaking into laughter after every few sentences. "And Marisol and I were the last ones to get off before the ride went amok. The people who were still on it were stuck for two hours, riding around and around."

He forced himself to laugh along with her. "Those poor people!" Oh, yeah, Raina, if you'd been on there, you wouldn't think it was so funny.

"We're not going back today, though," she said. "We want to have lots of experiences on this trip, so we're going to move on."

"When?" he asked, feeling the headache worsen.

"We're gonna hang around the pool here for a bit, then get going after lunch."

"And where are you heading?"

Now she sounded annoyed. "I don't think I'll tell you. Duff, sometimes I don't like it that you want to keep track of every minute of my life. We'll let you know when we get there...maybe."

He attempted to lighten the mood. "Not every minute, Raina. Every hour will do fine."

He heard Marisol say something in the background. "Say 'hi' to Marisol for me."

"I will. She wants to go to the pool now, so bye!" Before he had time to sign off with his usual "Love ya!" she was gone.

He called his mom. "How's the weather in Maine?"

"Bright and sunny. The neighbors have brought enough food for any army. Casseroles, you know."

"What kind of casseroles?" he asked, remembering his conversation about that with Raina.

"Well...chicken and biscuits, rice and beans, some sort of stew...I think venison. Or maybe moose. I haven't got up the nerve to try that yet."

He laughed. "I'd like that. Venison is delicious."

She laughed along with him, then changed the subject. "Michael, I'm glad you called. I'm busy getting the house in shape and working with the realtors, and it'll be a while. There's really no reason for you to hurry to get here. Take your time—sightsee a bit."

He knit his brow. "Really, Mom? I thought you needed me to sign all kinds of documents and stuff."

"There is a lot to do, but when I'm finished here, I can take the documents home to Stockbridge, and Kent Bridges—remember him from high school? He can work them out with us."

"Wow! Kent's a lawyer now?" Duff remembered the tall thin, red-headed boy who had been a few years ahead of him. At the same time, he felt a prickle of insecurity. What was he doing working in some doofy office in Florida, achieving nothing with his life? Well, there was Raina. That was the reason he was still there.

His mother, as usual, was a jump ahead of him. "Don't worry, Michael. You're going to get that job at Simon's Rock. I feel it in my bones."

"I hope that's all you feel in your bones," he joked. "But I called to tell you my car is in the garage, and may be there another day, so I can't get back on the road tomorrow."

"That's fine. Michael. I know how you love to stop and see things along the way, so take your time and enjoy yourself. I'll see you when you get here. By the way, Tanya is anxious to see you. She lit up like a one-hundred-watt bulb when I told her you were coming home."

"Oh, well, that's another story," he said, and rang off before his mother could ask what he meant by that.

Fourteen

"You missed breakfast," Candee's mom said, scowling at him. "It was 'specially good this morning."

"Sorry," Duff apologized as he paid his bill. "Overslept." He wasn't sorry at all. He knew his roiling stomach never could have tolerated a Blue Vision breakfast that morning.

Duff's car was ready, and Ted picked him up and drove him back to the service station. He listened absently as Ernie threw a lot of technical information at him, and charged the payment to his account.

He hopped in the car, glad to be on his way, especially if by accident he might run into Raina and Marisol. He went through the drive-thru at the McDonald's across the street and ordered a strawberry milkshake. He sat in the car and pondered what route to take to head north. The picnic in the meadow had taken him off route 95, and he didn't even know why he'd headed for Orlando, rather than staying straight north. He could cut over toward St. Augustine, then Jacksonville and over the border to Georgia.

The strawberry shake tasted surprisingly good. Hmmm. *Now I'm living Raina's life, Magic Kingdom and breakfast at McDonald's.* "Want a taste, S.B.? That's what I'll call you...Esbee." Playfully, he offered Sleeping Beauty a sip, then endured an incredulous look from a grandma-type walking by the car. She had scraggly white hair and wore a bright green matching top and slacks outfit. She stopped and rapped on the window.

He rolled it down, feeling foolish.

"Are you sure you're okay to drive, Sonny?"

"Yes, I'm fine, thank you."

"You haven't been drinking, have you?"

"It's ten o'clock in the morning. Just the strawberry shake, see?" He held it up for her to see, feeling ridiculous.

"Some people are drunk at ten o'clock in the morning. Did you put anything in that, like rum or vodka? I know all the tricks."

He tired of the inquisition. "Look, ma'am, I don't want to be rude, but I need to get on the road. You're not a cop, are you?"

Her face tightened and he immediately regretted asking that.

She grinned. "Retired, but I still know some people I could call. Are you sure you're all right? Let me smell your breath." She leaned forward.

He choked. "No thanks, ma'am. I'll be on my way now." He pressed the button that raised the window, and she snatched her hand away just in time. She shook a long, crooked finger at him. Duff set his shake in the cup holder, started the car and pulled out of the lot. She stood there like a bright green shrub, watching him, her hands on her waist.

He sipped his shake as he drove, cutting across the state toward St. Augustine and Interstate 95. The strawberry milkshake tasted surprisingly good. It was the first time he had ordered anything from McDonald's since he was a kid, except for the hamburger the night he'd arrived. Even then, he'd stopped going about eleven years of age, as he started developing an interest about more complex foods. He liked learning to cook, too, and his grandma heartily encouraged him. As he grew into his teens, the family would enjoy "French Night," or "Greek Night," and as he ventured further into more exotic foods, they had "Thai Night" and "Nigerian Night." He had never cooked for Raina, but had tried to 'educate' her by taking her to ethnic restaurants. She'd never really enjoyed any of them, though. Just take her to Outback, and she was in heaven. He sighed. He loved her, but their worlds were so far apart.

He looked at Sleeping Beauty, sitting up in the passenger seat. "What do you think, Esbee? How are we ever going to make it work, even if she does decide to give me a chance?"

Fifteen

Although it was out of his way, he decided to spend the night in St. Augustine, a city he loved. Due to his late start, it was near dinnertime as he approached the city limits.

He'd been there several times, loved the arty little shops, the old houses, the crooked streets. He looked at his watch. He remembered a wonderful restaurant right on the beach—just cross the bridge from the old town and drive along the beach road. He hoped it was still there.

And it was: Le Francais. Perhaps a little more time-worn, a bit shabbier. But with the ocean blazing blue behind it, and the white terraces that overlooked the water, he could tell it was still a popular place. He parked the car in the lot and wandered toward the back of the building. He wasn't all that hungry yet, and there were benches where visitors could sit and just enjoy the view. The beach, the sailboats, the glistening water.

And, he thought, given the direction the girls had taken, there would be no possibility of running into them there. Unless, he thought suddenly, unless they had planned on St. Augustine as one of their stops. He would just have to keep an eye peeled for them. Ouch! When you thought about that, it sounded painful.

"Madame Raina, I adore you, but I don't know how we're ever going to bring our lives together." But—other people had done it, and with enough compromise on both sides, he and Raina could do it too.

He shot to his feet as Raina and Marisol appeared, walking along the boardwalk toward the restaurant. Terrified at being spotted, he jumped behind a convenient tree—one of those twisted trees with long, spreading limbs, and roots and limbs growing over and disguising everything—and watched as they continued on, passing L'Francais. He saw Marisol look at the restaurant and gesture toward it, but Raina brushed her off with a negative wave of the hand, and they continued on. Duff shook his head, hardly able to believe it as they headed into a Denny's half a block away. When they did indeed turn in there, he sighed, not envying them their feast at Denny's, but envious that she would not be at this excellent restaurant, sharing a superlative meal with him. The empty feeling in his gut was not from hunger, but from missing Raina, and the chance to share a wonderful experience with her.

Oh, Raina, you really are just driving me crazy.

He resumed his seat on the bench, wondering if he should stay and eat or drive on toward Jacksonville, where he could no doubt find a good restaurant. But he didn't personally know of any there. "Should I stay and eat at Le Francais?"

"I would, if I were you. It's excellent."

He jumped, as the elderly woman in a red-flowered dress, sitting on the bench next to him, answered him. Lost in his own thoughts, he hadn't noticed her there. Had she been there when he sat down, or had she joined him later?

He looked at her. How had he not noticed her? He continued to look at her, thinking she looked just a tiny bit familiar. But, no, he decided. She looked like everyone's grandma.

"Uhm, yeah, I know," he admitted. "But I haven't eaten there in years. Just thought I'd make a return visit, see if it's as good as it used to be."

She nodded. "It is, and you have good taste then. I could use some company if you're not meeting someone else."

He glanced at her. She had to be eighty, if a day. Maybe eighty-five. Lots of character wrinkles. Her flowered dress had a white lace collar, and she had a little red bow in her hair. She looked like a throwback from fifty years ago. An aged Donna Reed or Doris Day, and appeared as if she couldn't handle a meal at Denny's, let alone some place fancier.

He struggled to be polite, as his mother had taught him, but he didn't want to have dinner with Grandma tonight. And if he ate dinner there it would be too late to get back on the road. And Raina and Marisol were there, despite his attempts to avoid them. Raina would be upset if she spotted him. Fate was just playing dirty tricks on him.

"Uh, I don't know, ma'am. Maybe I should get back on the road—"

She clucked. "If you don't need to go, you shouldn't. I've heard there's a roadblock on ninety-five, security check or something. Nothing's moving. You'd do best to eat and stay overnight here." She smiled at him. "I have a room at the Marriot there. The room has a balcony looking right out on the ocean. It's beautiful at night, the kind of view you want to take photographs to remember it by."

OMG! Does she think that if I eat dinner with her I'm going to spend the night with her, too?

She stood up and extended her hand to him. "Come on. I haven't had dinner with a handsome young man in quite a while. I'd really enjoy that."

He felt trapped. "Well, thank you, but I—"

"Oh, I'd love that!" The little old lady was on her feet right beside him. She offered him her arm. "Let's go."

"Oh, no, I didn't mean that—" He struggled for the right words. He didn't want to eat dinner with this woman who was older than his deceased Maine grandmother, and he sure didn't want to have to pay for her meal at Le Francais.

She about reached his breastbone. She looked up a him, her bright bird-like eyes twinkling. "Come on. The food there is excellent. It will be so nice to have a gentleman escort again. It's been a long time."

She latched onto his arm and started moving forward.

He stumbled. She was a lot stronger than she looked. *Oh, go on, Duff. Give a lonesome old lady one last thrill.*

The hostess welcomed them with a courtly bow. "Where would you and your grandmother like to sit? We have some nice tables in the bay windows."

"Oh, I'm not his grandmother," she chirped. "I'm his girlfriend."

"That would be fine," Duff said, with as much dignity as he could muster, trying to ignore the host's incredulous stare.

Once they were seated at a lovely table covered with a white linen tablecloth, set with candles and a bouquet of real flowers in the center, a waiter, tall, dark and impeccably handsome, appeared.

He looked down his nose at Duff. "May I suggest a fine wine for your dining pleasure?"

Grandma spoke up instead. "We'll have a bottle of Nozzoli's Chiante Classico.

Duff swallowed hard. He had only seen this wine on menus at the most high-end restaurants. The price of a bottle of that would cover a visit to the dentist! Duff began to protest, but she held up her hand. "I know what I'm doing, dear. Just relax."

I'll bet! This dinner date is going to wind up costing me three hundred dollars, and I walked right into this trap. But I can't walk out on her, I just can't. She'd be washing dishes here for a month.

The waiter stalked off to fetch the wine.

Duff felt he might as well introduce himself. "I'm Michael Duffy, Duff for short."

"I'm Myrtle," she replied and smiled at him. Perfect teeth—they had to be false.

Of course it's Myrtle. No surprise there. Did she have a last name? Duff shrugged. Did it matter? He'd never see her again.

She smiled again. "I'm visiting my daughter for a while." She paused, as if wondering whether or not to go on. "I'm taking some pictures of the ocean. It's sort of a hobby of mine."

He wondered what kind of camera she used. *Naw. I bet she's one of those people who are stuck in the past, still using those drugstore instamatics.*

Before he could ask, the waiter returned with the wine, and set two crystal goblets in front of each place. Duff gasped. "They're Waterford!"

"Yes, they do a nice job here," Myrtle said.

The waiter poured a little wine into Duff's glass and offered it to him to taste.

"Do you like it, darling?" Myrtle asked, a little smile on her lips. "If it doesn't suit you, we can order something better."

Duff took a sip. The wine was so smooth, so silky, so much better than anything he'd ever tasted, he didn't have the words to describe it.

"It's fine, it's fine, it's perfect," he managed.

"Now," Myrtle said to the waiter, "we'll start off with escargot."

"Very well." The waiter bowed again.

Duff gulped. *That'll be fifty dollars, at least.*

"And for your entrees?" The waiter posed, pad in hand.

"I'm not very hungry—" Duff began, but Myrtle laughed and cut him off.

"Oh, yes he is. These young men, they need to keep up their nutrition for all the things they're asked to do." She cocked a suggestive eyebrow at him. "Isn't that true, sweetheart?"

He wanted to sink into the floor. He stared at the table top, knowing his face was on fire.

Myrtle placed the order. "Boeuf Bourguignon for my darling boy, and I'll have *table de lievre a la crème—*"

Duff choked. *Rabbit? This old lady was going to eat rabbit?*

"And for dessert?" Mr. Handsome waited, his pencil poised. "*Le negre* is particularly delectable tonight."

Myrtle shook her head. "I think my love has probably eaten enough chocolate cake. We'll have *Tarte au fromage blanc.* And coffee, of course. Oh, and bring another bottle of this wine. I want this to be a special evening."

*So do I. But not with you, and not for what this is going to cost. My mom was right; never talk to strangers. But—*he was trapped. He might as well relax and enjoy the meal, and the ambiance.

As if reading his mind, Myrtle asked, "How do you like the paintings on the walls? They're all originals, you know, not prints or reproductions. Are you familiar with any of these artists?"

For once he was in his own territory. "Yes," he said. He pointed, but not too obviously. He'd been told by enough museum guards that paintings disliked being pointed at, and of course, you could never, ever touch one. "That one's a Renoir, and over there a Monet. Those two on that wall are both Sisley, and that one—"he gestured to a small painting near the corner, "is a Degas, of course, the ballet dancers—"

She interrupted, obviously pleased. "Well, you do know your art. So many of the young men I pick up are totally ignorant of fine art. If they know anyone, it's Rockwell or Wyeth."

"Or Kinkaid," Duff added. His least favorite artist, but of course Raina loved him. Naturally.

Suddenly Duff had a weird feeling that this old lady was not who she seemed to be. "Myrtle, what's your background?"

She waved her hand at him, negating his question. "Oh, let's not bother with trivia on this wonderful evening, darling. You make me feel young again, and I want to enjoy all this wonderful food. Here's our escargot."

Duff took one whiff of the butter, herbs and garlic, and thought he had gone to heaven. All at once he didn't care who he was with or how much the meal cost him. This was obviously the one of the finest, if not the finest, French restaurants he had ever visited. Myrtle wanted to enjoy the food, and he was up for that.

When they had finished the meal, the second bottle of wine, and the luscious cheese tart with *café au lait*, Duff settled back and gazed at Myrtle. "This is the best meal I've ever eaten in my life. Probably the best I ever will eat."

"I'm glad you enjoyed it," she said. "I think it's good for young people to get a taste of real food, real culture. You'll never feel the same about a Big Mac again."

"I never have felt the same about a Big Mac," he said.

She picked up her shabby purse, worn red leather with a tear in the corner. "I need to visit the ladies' room. The waiter will be over to settle up." She stood up, leaned over and planted a kiss on his forehead. "I do hope this will be an evening you'll never forget."

Oh, I'll never forget it. Neither will my credit card company. He got his wallet out of his back pocket and took out his Visa. He sipped his coffee and waited for the waiter to come over, and for Myrtle to return.

Ten minutes later she had not come back. Fifteen, twenty. He might have known. After ordering an incredibly expensive meal, she had skipped out on him. Well, that was how everything else was going on this freakin' road trip.

Dumb! Dumb! Dumb!

The waiter stopped at the table, and looked at him curiously. "Will there be anything else, sir?"

"Well, I have to settle up for this." He extended the card.

The waiter smiled. "Oh, no, sir. Miss Simmons took care of that before she left. You're all set."

Simmons? Myrtle Simmons? Duff fell back into his chair. "That was Myrtle Simmons?"

"Yes, sir. She does that all the time. Likes to give the average guy a taste of fine dining. She brings a lot of young men in here. Says it makes her feel young again, like she's out on a date for the first time." He smiled at Duff and went on his way.

Duff put his face in his hands and his head down on the table. The emotions that swept through him ranged from embarrassment to humility to exaltation. It was as if he'd been privileged to have dinner with Marc Chagall or Pablo Picasso. He had just spent an evening dining with Myrtle Simmons! And after Ansel Adams, she was just the most famous landscape photographer in the world, that's who she was.

Sixteen

He couldn't wait to tell Raina, he just couldn't wait! He hadn't booked himself into a motel before dinner, and now he needed a place to crash for the night. He realized the classy Marriot right on the beach was where the girls were probably staying, so he got back in his car and drove a mile or so down the street. He stopped at the Ocean View. Small and rather shabby...he would never run into them here.

I only need to spend one night here. But at least I'll have a view of the ocean.

The young guy behind the counter had scraggly hair and a shaggy moustache with about nine hairs in it, and was rail thin. He looked like an emaciated Hitler. His nametag said 'Jem.' Duff supposed from his experience with Candee, that Jem probably pronounced his name Jame or Jime, or maybe with a Spanish J sound, Wem. Like Juan. Or Hem—like Jose.

Jem handed over the key card without saying anything.

Duff hurried back to his room, and found that while three sides of the building had ocean views, his room faced the street. The walls were beige, the listless drapes were beige, and the carpet was....or used to be...beige. Two of those big-eyed kids prints hung on the walls.

Duff went into the bathroom and pulled two of the towels from the towel rack. He draped them over the paintings he found to be just too cute, too sentimental. The white surfaces suited him better, even if it did leave him without a towel.

He pulled out his cell phone and flopped in the chair by the window. What a story he had to tell! Even the dreary motel couldn't dampen his mood.

He pressed in Raina's number.

"Hi, Duff! We're downtown in St. Augustine. There's a street dance tonight—"

He heard Marisol hiss behind her, "Raina! He's at a funeral! Empathy!"

She broke off, and her voice took on her mournful tone. "But how are you? I've been thinking about you and what you must be going through. It's just so hard, isn't it?"

He deflated as if he were a huge balloon, losing all its air at once. He couldn't tell her about his amazing evening. He couldn't even pretend it had happened in Maine. What business would he have eating out at a pricey French restaurant with a world-famous photographer when he was supposed to be comforting his grieving family?

"Where are you staying in St. Augustine?" Bet it's not the Ocean View without an ocean view.

"What does that matter?" she asked. Her voice gentled. "Let's just talk about you. It must be so difficult."

"Well," he said, pretending to put on a brave front, "let's not talk about me. We're doing the best we can here. We weren't that close to Granny Tyler. There's just a lot of legal stuff to work out, and about the house and all. By the way, the old lady left me a brand new Lexus. What do you think of that?"

"Oh," she said, her voice on a downswing, "we always get Chevies or Fords. What's the sense of spending all the money on something like a Lexus? A car is to get you from one place to another, right?"

Duff cleared his throat and changed the subject. "What are you and Marisol up to tonight?"

She let her voice show more enthusiasm. "There's a street festival in downtown St Augustine tonight...dancing, food, a band—everything! We had to get advance tickets for this, as they're limiting the number of people who can attend. We're in our room changing now, and we're going to get a bus that goes over that long beach to town instead of driving, and—"

"You be careful," Duff interrupted. "Anyone can take a bus, you know. There can be unsavory characters on a bus, drifters, and um, other undesirables."

She laughed and he heard her repeat what he'd said to Marisol.

Marisol came on the line, sounding amused. "Duff, you're much too protective of her. She's a grown-up woman. We know enough to not to take up with 'unsavory' characters."

"Yes, but you're going downtown at night..."

"Duff," she said, a note of exasperation in her voice, "it's not Chicago, not even Miami. They have chartered buses to take us there and back. We'll be fine."

"I know," he admitted. "I worry about her too much. Are you having a good time together, getting in some good talks and all?"

"Yes, that's true. We've been having some good talks."

She lowered her voice almost to a whisper. "Duff, she's in the bathroom now. I'm really trying to talk to her about your relationship, and how she should give you more of a chance."

He was surprised. "Oh, really? That's great of you, Marisol. You know, I'm nuts about her. I know she's the girl for me. I just have to convince her of it."

"I think you'd be good for her. She's a smart girl. I'm trying to get her to see the light."

Gratitude overwhelmed him. "Thanks so much, Marisol. When I think about that, it will make it so much easier to be here, making all these funeral arrangements. It's something I hope I never have to do again."

"I guess we all have to sometime or another. Well, she's ready now, so I'd better hang up and get ready, too. You have a good evening. Say hello to your mother for us."

"I will." He clicked his phone off, feeling hopeful and relieved. Marisol was a good friend. She had sometimes hinted that she would like the concerts and plays and art exhibits to which he took Raina, but his heart was hers, and he couldn't help that.

He lay back on his bed. If the buses were commissioned specially for the street festival, it was probably going to be monitored. He put his arms around Sleeping Beauty. It felt so good to have someone in his arms, even if it wasn't Raina.

He flicked the TV on and lowered the volume. He'd catch up on the world and local news, and take a break from the fictional news from Maine.

Seventeen

"Which house do you like, Raina, the yellow colonial or the green cape?" He held her hand as they walked through the streets of Pontoosuc Pointe, the brand new gated enclave set above the lake of the same name in the Berkshire hills of western Massachusetts.

She patted her stomach. The baby didn't show yet, but would by the time they moved into their new house. "I sort of like the cape. It's really cute, and I can picture us living there."

"They're both available," he said, bending down protectively over her. "The real estate lady showed us both of them. More space in the colonial if we end up having a big family."

She laughed. "I think two will be plenty for me. And, being from Florida, I'm not used to running up and down stairs. I like one level better."

"Then we'll make it final tomorrow." He looked down at her, feeling so much love. At last she was his, and their baby was on the way. He had secured a position at Simon's Rock, a prestigious high school-college combination institute, and everything was falling into place.

He woke slowly with a feeling of warmth and total contentment. He pictured Raina's face as he had seen it in his dream. He hadn't meant to fall asleep. Was the dream a glimpse of their future together? Did this mean he didn't have to get so worked up about Raina and whether she would ever love him as he loved her? He fluffed up his pillow and sat back against it, taking care to place Esbee on her own side of the bed.

The details of the dream were fast disappearing from his memory, but the warm feelings of excitement and hopes for the future lingered. Restless, he flicked on the television, and ran through the list of available movies to watch. Nothing appealed to him. But he couldn't go into town and visit the arty little places he remembered because the girls were going to the street festival.

How about a movie in an actual theatre? He wasn't going to run into them there. In the dark. With a Coke and stale popcorn. Not exciting, but he just couldn't sit around that drab, claustrophobic room.

He retraced his steps to the motel office. Young Mr. Moustache was there, looking bored. He shifted a vague look to Duff. "Hep ya?"

"Where is the nearest movie theatre?"

Jem, Yem, Wem, Jime, Jeme looked at the clock on the wall without shifting his head a micro-inch. "Just over the bridge. Turn right and go about a block. The Royal. But there's a street festival tonight and the bridge will prob'ly be all clogged up."

Duff didn't stop to ask any more questions. He dashed to the parking lot and ran toward his car. As he jammed the key into the lock, and it refused to open, he realized it was the same color and model, but not his vehicle. Where was his car? He looked around, confused, for a few paralyzing seconds before he spotted his own vehicle. Hmmm. Things seemed to be happening in twos lately. Two identical red Focuses, two battered black Toyotas. He shook his head, amused at himself. For a guy who was supposed to be so smart, he certainly did some stupid things sometimes.

Dumb, dumb, dumb.

He put his key in the ignition, drove down the main street, and within minutes was on the long bridge that separated the island from the mainland.

The shabby brown Jeep ahead of him had a dent in its fender, and it seemed to have slowed down, for no reason he could guess. Suddenly the driver stuck his head out of the window, looked back, yelled something and made the third-finger gesture.

"What?" Duff reduced his speed as the brown car slowed.

The car behind him, a silver Honda, honked his horn.

Duff turned in his seat, confused. Couldn't the doofus see he couldn't go anywhere? He wasn't the one slowing down and holding up the whole procession.

The Jeep slowed even more, and Duff had no choice but to slow behind it.

He felt a jolt as the Honda nudged his bumper. From his rear-view mirror, Duff saw the angry face of the driver, shouting something.

How was he the problem? He flicked on his directional, and looked for a way to edge into the other lane, but the other drivers weren't having any of that. As the cars passed he received a variety of reactions, from children staring at him from their windows and laughing, to drivers shaking their heads or fists.

One middle-aged woman, fake blonde with a round face and earrings down to her shoulders, leaned out her window and yelled, "Wait your turn, bub!"

The Jeep stopped. Duff stepped on the brake as hard as he could and yanked the wheel to the right, but it wasn't fast enough to keep him from nudging the back of the vehicle in front of him.

Duff locked the car door as the Jeep's driver jumped from his car, a look of utter fury on his face.

"Oh, my God! What did I get myself into?" *What would Superman do now, Dufus? Shoulda stayed in bed.*

The man, a beefy guy past middle age, wearing jeans and a tee that said, 'Revolution Now!' ran toward him. With both relief and panic, Duff realized he was not the cause or the target. The driver of the Honda met Mr. Revolution right outside Duff's window, and a loud yelling match ensued.

Twenty cars behind them began honking their horns.

Duff leaned on the steering wheel, his head in his hands. What now? All he wanted was to cross the bridge into town and see some time-wasting movie, but these two jerks didn't care if they held everybody else up, as long as they had some score to settle.

Mr. Jeep took a swing at Mr. Honda, who reeled back, but recovered in time to deck Mr. Jeep in the chin. Mr. Jeep went down, but grabbed Mr. Honda's leg and brought him to the pavement as well. Suddenly a third man walked up from behind. He wore a gray suit, white shirt and tie, and looked as though he were late for a business meeting.

"Hey, guys, can you settle this somewhere else? Traffic is backed up all the way to the island."

The Honda owner turned on him and floored him with one blow. Mr. Gray Suit sat on the pavement, rubbing his chin, as two more men ran up and tried to stop the fighting.

The Honda driver dragged Mr. Jeep to his feet and pinned him against the door of Duff's car. Mr. Graysuit struggled to his feet and attacked the third man from behind.

Duff rolled his window down about six inches. "Hey, could you guys take your fight somewhere else? I gotta get across this bridge sometime tonight, and—"

"Stay outta this!" the Jeep driver yelled., fury turning his face crimson.

Several other men joined the group, trying to intervene so traffic could get moving again, but the melee just grew worse. The noise from the blaring horns woke Duff's headache again. Then he heard the sirens, and from the opposite direction came the lights and sirens at full blast.

The police seemed in no hurry to clear the bridge, as they cuffed the drivers of the Jeep and the Honda, and began interrogating the others involved.

The taller cop knocked on Duff's window. He rolled it down. "License, registration and insurance card, please."

Duff fumbled with his wallet to produce the information. "Listen, Officer, I was just sitting here. I had nothing to do with any of this."

The policeman nodded. "This is just the driver in front of you and the one in back of you, right? You're not involved at all, right?"

"Right."

"Step out of the vehicle, Mr. Duffy." The cop handed him back his cards.

The other policeman stared at him as Duff exited his car. "Who started this whole thing?"

Duff pointed at the burly, rough-looking fellow who had been driving the Jeep, and pointed a finger at him. "That one."

"Liar!" the man roared, glaring at Duff, and struggled to free himself from the cop's grasp. "He ran into my car—just look at it."

Everyone turned to look at the battered Jeep.

The man in the suit shook his head. "This young man had nothing to do with it. It was the guy in the Jeep and the one in the Honda who started it."

The cop looked at Duff and nodded. "You're the only one who doesn't look roughed up, so I tend to believe that." He opened the door of Duff's car. "You're not under arrest or anything, but you'll have to sit here while we take statements from everyone who saw anything, including you, and then we'll have to clear the bridge. So, just prepare yourself for a long wait."

"But—if I'm not under suspicion for anything, can't I go over to the mainland?"

"No, sir. We're going to close down traffic over the bridge. Everyone needs to go back to the island. The buses will begin loading in an hour or so to bring people back from the festival anyway, so we're going to close traffic in this direction."

Duff turned in his seat and watched as the officers held up traffic in the other lane, clearing a spot for the cars in back to turn around. Several other cruisers arrived and blocked the traffic ahead, forcing everyone to turn around and return to the island.

Two hours later, after giving his statement, he was allowed to back his auto into the other lane and head back in the direction he had come.

Duff stumbled into his motel room, exhausted. He fell onto the bed. Here it was, only Thursday, and he'd gotten into more trouble than the entire previous twenty-four years of his life.

West Palm was only six hours from St. Augustine, and it taken two days and two nights to get this far. And he kept bumping into Raina and her friend, no matter how hard he tried to avoid them. Maybe Dianne had laid a curse on him. This wasn't going well at all.

Eighteen

Early Thursday morning brought sudden severe thunderstorms, waking Duff and probably everyone else in the St. Augustine area. He pulled himself up to a sitting position, adjusted the pillows behind him and flicked on the TV.

"...and rain for the next several hours and chance of a tornado. Residents are advised to keep indoors until ten a.m., when the storm should have passed."

Duff sighed. No point heading for the interstate then. He'd look for a decent movie on the TV—which seemed most desirable after his frustrating experience on the bridge the night before—stay in bed until eight or so, then chance the motel breakfast if the weather were still bad. He felt depressed just thinking about the breakfast.

He alternately dozed and watched the movie while the storm raged.

The rain finally eased off, but didn't stop completely, and echoes of thunder still sounded from time to time. Duff reached for his phone. He'd check in on Raina, then decide what to do.

"Quite a storm!" he said when she picked up.

She sounded surprised. "Oh, are you having one in Maine, too? You should have been here. It was like world war three out there."

He scrambled to cover his error. "Oh, no, it's calm here...I just happened to turn on the national forecast." He changed the subject. "What are your plans today?"

"We aren't sure. Our motel's right on the beach. Breakfast included, you know how it is. I think it will clear up, and we'll just spend the day on the beach."

Duff threw his long legs over the side of the bed, got up and wandered over to the window. Lovely view of the street, streaked with water. "And if doesn't clear up?" he asked.

She laughed. "Then we'll definitely stay here. There's an indoor pool and exercise room. We don't want to drive in this."

Good! You stay there, and I'll leave and get out of your way. Stay another day and no way will you catch up with me.

"No, the streets look slippery, and you know how it is in Florida. You get a lot of rain and the roads flood."

"The streets look slippery?" she asked. "Are they showing this part of St. Augustine on the weather channel?" He heard her call out, "Marisol, put on the weather channel. Duff says they're showing our streets!"

Duff cast a look at the television. Blue skies and sunshine blazed over the fields in Kansas.

"No, they're not, Duff," she said in a puzzled tone. "They're showing the Midwest. Looks beautiful there."

"It just changed. They were showing your street. What motel are you at?"

"Marriot."

"Yeah, I saw it with my own eyes." That much was the truth, even if he hadn't seen it on the telly.

"How was the funeral?" she asked. "I'm sorry I didn't ask about that right away. Was it one of those sad ones, or was it more of a happy-memory kind of thing?"

He hedged. "Well, funerals are all sad, aren't they, when someone's died?"

"Well, it depends. If they've had a long, happy life and weren't too sick—how old was your grandmother, anyway?"

Duff rubbed a hand across his eyes. It was too early for this kind of questioning, too early for him to have to make up answers without even having had any coffee. And his special Kona coffee had run out. He would have to drink motel muck until he could get some more.

"Well?"

"Well what?"

"How old was she?"

"Ninety-one."

"And she hadn't really been sick?"

"No. This was very sudden."

"Well, there's no reason to be sad about her life then, is there?"

"No, I guess not, but everyone is very sad here anyway." He really wanted some coffee. "Listen, Raina, if you decide to go somewhere today, just give me a call, okay?"

There was a brief pause before she said, "Why?"

"Oh, you know me!" He forced a laugh. "I always need to keep tabs on you."

He knew immediately it was the wrong thing to have said.

Her voice became cool. "No, you don't. Duff. I haven't said anything about your calling me all the time, but I think you should cool it. I think we should cool it."

"Raina," he said, "I love you. I've told you that over and over. I had the best dream last night about our life together, after we're married—"

"Married!" Raina sputtered. "Duff, we're not even engaged, and we're not going to be. I'm not ready to get married. I want a vacation from love! You have to get over me."

He stared across the street. "No, I don't."

"Yes, you do. And you promised me you'd have two dates with other girls while I was gone, remember fhat?"

"I'll do it while I'm here, in Maine. I saw a couple of strapping young ladies the other day—sort of built like elks, but..."

She laughed, but he also heard an edge to Raina's voice. "When? At the funeral? At the reception dinner afterwards? I don't think so!"

"Raina," he pleaded. "I don't want to date anyone else."

"I don't want you to call me for three days," she said. "And if I see it's you, I'm not going to answer. You're crowding me just like you do at the office. One of the reasons I went on this road trip with Marisol was to get some space, Duff. I need time to think and space to breathe."

"Just tell me this," he pleaded. "Where are you going next, Atlanta maybe?"

"I don't know, Duff. We're playing it by ear."

"Are you going to go up ninety-five, or will you take another route?"

"I don't know!" She hung up.

He stared at the phone, glanced out the window at the dripping rain, and back at the phone. He sighed. "Oh, Raina. Just drivin' me nuts, sweet girl. You play it by ear, but I play it by eye, and you are all my eyes ever want to see."

Nineteen

Duff sat by the window, watching. He had no choice but to wait until the rain let up, but he was anxious to be off. Suddenly the rain did cease, the sky changed from gray to blue in fifteen minutes, as skies in Florida do, almost as if they are making an apology for the previous bad weather.

His coffee-addiction screamed at him and his stomach rumbled with hunger. He'd grab a quick meal, then get on the road. Oh, and he needed gas, too. Well, he'd fill up himself and the car, then come back for his things. He waved to his laptop and suitcase, which as usual, he had parked on the other bed. "Bye! Bye! I'm outta here to get something to eat." He bent and kissed Esbee on the top of her head, as she sat with her back against his pillow. "Back soon."

He'd noticed a sidewalk café down the street from Denny's, just past where he'd sat on the bench with Myrtle Simmons. His mood brightened. Maybe he would see her again, and this time he would be able to have a sensible conversation with her, about her photography, about art in general. If he ran into her, maybe she would have a book of her photographs she would sell him and autograph for him. That would be a treasure he would keep forever, and almost make up for how frustrating this trip had been.

He chose a table under the yellow and white striped awning, as far back from the sidewalk as he could get. He didn't think the girls would leave the motel, but he could easily duck into the restaurant if they came this way.

It was still early, and he wanted breakfast. He ordered an omelet stuffed with mushrooms and shrimp. When it came, hot and steaming, with an aroma that promised it would be as good as it looked, he tackled it with gusto.

He watched the tourists come and go, wishing he could openly be one of them, longing to be with Raina, enjoying this beautiful beach, exploring charming St Augustine, which claimed the honor of being the oldest city in the United States. He sighed. That would have to wait, but the day would come. It would.

He headed toward his motel. His eyes fell on the car, and he remembered how low the gas tank had registered, after the fiasco on the bridge. He would get the gas first, then go back, pick up his things, pay his bill and be on the road.

He prepaid for the gas and went out to fill the tank. Almost finished, he jumped as he heard a sudden loud crash behind him. He yanked the nozzle from the car, and wheeled around, holding the hose, his finger still pressing the trigger. Instantly, he was drenched, his shirt and shorts saturated with the spurting gasoline.

Two cars had hit each other, but it was just a fender bender for both, and nobody was hurt. The drivers got out and began to exchange information.

Duff looked down at his shirt and shorts, wet and reeking with the smell of gas.

"I can't believe I did that. Dumb! Dumb! Dumb!"

There was no option except to return to the motel, dispose of the clothing, take a shower, and change into something else. He looked into the car, hoping to find something to put on the driver's seat, so as not to soak the fabric with gasoline. There was nothing. He fished in his pockets for change, ran into the station, grabbed a newspaper and threw four quarters on the counter.

"Whoa!" gasped the clerk, jerking backwards as he got a whiff of Duff.

He spread the newspaper on the seat, hoping it would be enough to absorb the gas for the short ride back to the motel.

He chucked the newspaper in the nearest trash can as he ran up the stairs to his room. He passed several people, who drew back and stared at him with their mouths open as he dashed past them.

Inside his room, he peeled off his clothes and threw them on the floor. The shower felt wonderful, and he lingered, loving the feel of the hot water as it coursed over his body. He soaped up several times, and washed his hair, wanting to make sure the gas odor was washed out.

As he stood under the water, he had a sudden sense of something being wrong. A picture formed in his mind, and in an instant, he knew what it was.

"Oh, no! Oh, no, it can't be."

He groaned in dismay and jumped out of the shower, grabbed one of the face towels, trying to dry himself off as he went into the bedroom. He stared at the bed in total disbelief.

His suitcase and laptop were gone.

Esbee was still there, however. She gazed at him with her big blue eyes, but she had nothing to tell him.

Twenty

What to do? What to do? Naked, he ran around the room, hoping the maid had come in and cleaned, and put his suitcase and laptop away somewhere. No, the suitcase was not in the closet, and the laptop had not been secreted away in any of the bureau drawers. He looked under the bed, and everywhere else he could imagine something could be hidden. Nothing. All his possessions, including his crystal wine glasses, were just...gone.

Don't panic, don't panic, don't panic...he told himself, but that was certainly difficult, given the circumstances. He picked up the phone and pressed zero to contact the office.

"Ocean View Motel," Jem answered, already sounding bored.

"Jem, this is Michael Duffy in room two-eleven. I just got home from going out to breakfast, and my suitcase and laptop are missing."

"We have free breakfast for our guests right here," Jem said. "Don't you like our breakfasts?"

"Jem, that's not the point!"

"What is the point? It's an insult to us if you go out and pay for breakfast when you can get it free right here. If you don't like our breakfasts, you need to fill out a complaint form, and we'll do our best to—"

"Jem!" Duff didn't mean to yell, but his frustration had reached its boiling point. "Listen to me. This is not about breakfast!"

"You don't need to yell at me, Mr. Duffy." Jem's voice took on an injured tone. "I'll pass on your complaints about our breakfasts—"

Duff lost it. He shook the receiver, shouting into it. "Jem! This isn't about breakfast! Someone has come in here while I was gone, and taken my suitcase and laptop, damn it!"

"Oh. Sorry. I took a continuing education class once, you know the company provides those for us, free of charge, and I learned the first half dozen words in a sentence is usually what the customer's concern is actually about, so I didn't really listen to the rest of the sentence. Did you tell me about the suitcase and laptop before?"

Duff forced himself to calm down. "Yes, I did. All my clothes are gone. Does this motel have insurance to cover these losses?"

"Yes, it does. Fifty dollars. Why don't you come to the office and I'll give you a form to fill out. Of course, we can't just give you fifty dollars. There will have to be an investigation—"

"Fifty dollars! For a suitcase full of clothes and a laptop! That's criminal!" He heard his voice rising again, but he couldn't help it. This kid was useless.

"And it may take six months to a year for the company to reimburse you. Mr. Duffy, if you don't like our breakfasts, and our policies, I would suggest you stay somewhere else from now on."

"And I suggest you come to my room and verify that my possessions are gone."

A silence followed, and Duff heard hushed voices in the background as if a discussion with others were going on.

Finally Jem came back on the line. He sounded official, as if something had interrupted the boredom of the day. "All right, Mr. Duffy, I will be there directly, to search the premises myself. I'll bring both forms for you to fill out."

"Both forms? What do you mean, both forms?"

Jem sighed, as if he thought Duff terminally obtuse. "The one for the insurance payment, and the breakfast complaint form."

Duff passed a hand over his eyes, backed up and sat on the bed. "Great." he replaced the receiver. This was just unbelievable, that his laptop and suitcase were missing, but all the clerk seemed to be able to think about was that he hadn't had breakfast there.

He suddenly realized he had no clothes on. He jumped up and tore a towel from one of the Big Eyes, wrapped it around his waist and tucked in one end. He hoped it would stay tucked in. With his luck running the way it had been, and Jem in the room with him—well, he didn't need that kind of problem.

He wheeled around as the knock on the door sounded. He ran across the room and yanked it open.

Jem entered, looking younger and more scraggly than ever. His face took on a suspicious expression as he looked at Duff. He took a few steps backwards. "Why aren't you dressed, Mr. Duffy?"

"I told you," Duff said, gritting his teeth and trying for patience. "My suitcase—and my laptop—are missing. I have no clothes."

Jem pointed to the gas-soaked shorts, shirt and underwear that lay puddled on the floor. "What's that?"

"I spilled gas on them when I filled up my tank at the station. Look, Jem, would you just take a look around and verify that my stuff isn't here?"

"Well...okay, but..uh, Mr. Duffy, would you go sit in that chair by the window, please, while I look?" He placed the two official forms he'd brought with him on the desk.

Duff flashed him a puzzled look. "Why?"

Jem looked embarrassed. "Well...uh, I wouldn't want you to get any ideas, Mr. Duffy...about me, that is. I know I'm small and cute and look young for my age, but I—"

"Oh, God!" Duff didn't know whether to laugh or cry. "Jem, you have no worries whatsoever about that. My girlfriend is staying at the motel right up the street."

He knew immediately it was the wrong thing to have said.

Jem's eyes narrowed and his face screwed up into even more of an untrusting look.

"No, you don't! That's not the way it is." However, he had no intention of trying to explain anything else to Jem. The kid took everything the wrong way. He retreated to the chair by the window. "I'll just sit here. Go check everything out, will you?"

Jem reluctantly began to search the room, opening bureau and desk drawers, looking into the closet. He kept a wary eye on Duff as he prowled around the room. His eyes went to the towel-covered artwork, and he shot a curious glance at Duff, but didn't say anything.

"Be sure to check under the beds," Duff reminded him.

Jem looked even more scared as he got down on his hands and knees to do that. He jumped to his feet after briefly checking both beds. He pointed to the two papers he had dropped onto the desktop. "Just fill those out, sir, and return them to me when you check out." He looked at his watch. "It's after eleven, so you'll have to pay for another day."

"What?" Duff stood, and Jem backed toward the door. "After all this, my luggage and laptop are stolen, and I have to pay for another day when I won't even be here?"

"Regulations, sir." Jem pointed to the pile of clothes on the carpet. "I guess you'll have to put those back on, until you can get something else to wear."

Duff sighed. "Is there are Walmart or a Target close?"

Jem thought, then seemed to have a burst of inspiration. "No, sir, but just over the bridge, if you take a left, go about a quarter of a mile, there's a great Goodwill. That's where I get my clothes."

Duff stared at him in disbelief.

Jem brightened and smiled, as if he'd done Duff a tremendous favor. "Just fill out the forms and I'll see you at check-out." He closed the door behind him.

"You'll not only see me, you'll smell me, too." Duff picked up the stinking bundle of clothes, which were wrinkled as well as reeking with the gas odor, and proceeded to get dressed again.

He completed the two forms and left his room, going down the stairs and along the corridor to the front office, where he completed his check-out. Several people waiting for service shrank back at the sight of him, and hurriedly retreated to the other side of the lobby.

"Thank you, sir," Jem said with careful courtesy. "Would you just mind answering one question for me?"

"Sure," Duff answered. "What is it?"

"Well, why did your girlfriend, if this isn't a stalking thing, stay across the street and you stayed here? That doesn't make any sense to me."

Duff stared at the pimply young face with its nine-hair Hitler moustache. He just couldn't resist.

"Oh," he said in an off-hand manner, "she doesn't like the breakfast here."

He turned on his heel and left the Ocean View.

Twenty-one

"Well, at least the gas tank is full." There was always an upside to everything. "And, I had my wallet, my money, my credit cards and all that with me. That's the good news. And they didn't steal Esbee." He started to laugh as he turned the car onto the bridge. He couldn't stop laughing, and he laughed all the way across the long span, sometimes collapsing against the steering wheel. Drivers in the other lane passed him, and shot him puzzled, sometimes irate looks, as he doubled up over the steering wheel.

When he departed the bridge, he turned left as Jem had instructed him, and sure enough, within a quarter of a mile, there was a large Goodwill store—in fact, it had 'Goodwill Boutique" in good-sized letters across the front.

Inside the store, it was surprisingly neat, clean, and the merchandise was displayed attractively in rows, although it still had that thrift-store scent. He knew he smelled bad, and looked, worse. People shied away from him, casting disgusted looks in his direction as he roamed the aisles. He went first to 'Mens' Shirts.' He selected two dress shirts, which did look almost new, went on to the tees, shorts and a pair of Dockers, as well as a pair of darker dress pants.

He also located swim trunks, pajamas, a short terry robe, and a couple of beach towels. He picked up a Miami Dolphins jacket, and a navy pullover sweater, in case he headed into colder weather. He fingered a navy blazer with gold buttons...would he need something like this before he got back home? He tossed in onto the pile.

He cringed at the idea of wearing second hand socks and underwear, but he didn't want to take the time to shop elsewhere, so he threw a handful of each into the cart. In another department, he found a suitcase, which was actually nicer than the one he'd had. He took his loot and headed for the check-out counter.

The woman ahead of him turned around, looked at him, sniffed and said, "Oh my gracious goodness, I forgot something." She wheeled her cart out of line and headed toward the back of the store.

The clerk looked at his credit card closely and wrinkled her nose. "You're sure this hasn't expired, or anything, has it?"

"It's good," he said, not wanting to get into the whole story.

"Just a minute, sir," she said, as she took his card and went off into the store. The three people behind him heaved weary, restless sighs.

She came back with a rotund, panting gentleman wearing a shiny brown suit.

He looked at Duff, taking note of his clothes. "May we see some other form of identification, sir?"

Duff dug out his license, and handed it to him.

"Do you have anything else?"

"Here's my library card," Duff said, "and, uh, my season pass to the Florida Ballet."

The man looked at the pass, obviously trying not to laugh. "Yes, sir, I'm sure you enjoy the ballet." He doubled over, laughing. "Is that what you're buying these clothes for...to attend the ballet?"

To the clerk he said, "Everything seems to be in order. Nothing we can do about it. Check him out."

"Yes, Mr. Ellis." She proceeded to ring up his purchases. The total came to twenty-six dollars and forty-five cents. She handed him back his credit card.

Duff fled the store. Once in the car he looked around for a secluded spot, and picked one at the far end of the parking lot. He stopped the car on one side of a huge dumpster, hoping that would hide him from prying eyes while he changed clothes inside the car. Several large pines shaded the area in front of him.

He tore off his crumpled, gas-soaked shirt and threw it on the floor with disgust. He supposed he still smelled like gasoline, but thrift-store odor wouldn't be quite so bad. He dumped all the new, second-hand clothing out of the bag onto the passenger seat. Esbee's head poked out from the top of the pile. He selected a green and white striped tee, and slipped it over his head.

He began to wriggle out of his shorts and briefs, but that proved to be a more difficult task in a close space with a steering wheel in front of him.

A police car cruised around the store, slowed down, but then continued on its way.

Duff breathed a sigh of relief. Who knows what it looked like he was doing, flailing around in the seat, his head bobbing, and his body jerking up and down. He got the lower garments off and threw them on top of the shirt. Grimacing, he drew on a pair of briefs, and followed them with khaki shorts. Just as he pulled his shirt down over them, there came a tap at the window, and there was the cop, signaling for him to roll down the window.

Duff rolled down the window.

He was a young officer, fresh-faced and earnest-looking. "What are you doing back here, sir?" He looked like he was having trouble getting the 'sir' past his lips.

Duff gestured to the pile of clothing. "I just bought clothes in there, in the Goodwill store, because my suitcase got stolen at my motel. I'm packing them in my new suitcase."

The policeman looked at the suitcase and the pile of clothing. "Do you have a receipt for all that?"

Duff remembered stuffing the receipt in the gassy-smelling shorts. He leaned over and picked them up from the floor. He pulled out the balled-up slip of paper, and smoothed it out the best he could.

The officer looked at it, and at the pile of clothes, evidently trying to match up the items. Anticipating the next request, Duff took out his license, his credit card, his library card and his ballet pass.

The officer nodded and handed back his receipt. "Well, you know it just looked sort of suspicious to me. I saw you sort of wrestling around in the seat, and I thought it just might be you were forcing yourself on someone, or—"

"No, no, no!" Duff protested. "I just needed to—"

The cop cut him off. "Yeah, I know, there are times we just have to relieve ourselves. I know how it is, and that's not a crime, but it's not a good thing to do in public, either. Just watch where you are when you do that."

He gave Duff a wave and headed off to the cruiser.

Duff sat frozen to his seat, staring straight ahead as he digested the cop's meaning. He didn't know whether to laugh, or die from humiliation right there in his battered old Toyota.

Then, biting his lip, he very meticulously folded each item of clothing and packed it away in his new suitcase. He got out of the car and threw his old clothes into the dumpster. He started up the car and drove out of the lot. The young officer had parked by the entry road. He gave Duff a toot of his horn and a friendly wave as he drove past.

Twenty-two

Duff cut across the necessary roads and headed toward Interstate 95. He didn't know when, and if or where the girls were going, but it made the most sense for them to head north. What would they be most likely to stop and see next? The Golden Isles were interesting, and the Okeefenokee Swamp would be mega-interesting to him, but he didn't really think Raina would find that much of a draw. Black water, alligators, snakes—yuk. Not Raina's type of thing. And he couldn't call Raina and find out where she was for two days yet.

His mom had said he could take his time, sightsee if he wanted to. What did he want to do? So far his adventures weren't turning out so well—except for Myrtle Simmons, that is. That was a memory he would treasure for a lifetime.

Savannah? That seemed to be the most logical choice. That was an old, historical city with beautiful old homes and many other attractions. Maybe they would visit a plantation. Okay, at all costs he would avoid Savannah. He could probably make it to North Carolina if he drove straight on and didn't get sidetracked. In a couple of hours he crossed into Georgia. The palm trees thinned out, the forest, heavy with firs, took over. Georgia had its own smell...partly the fresh, lush scent of the pines, partly the heavy, rancid smell of the pig farms. It wasn't a state you wanted to drive through with the windows down. Even with the windows closed and the air-conditioning on, the odor couldn't be eliminated completely.

All the radio stations offered talk show hosts ranting about their particular point of view, and country singers, lamenting their loss of wife, dog, home, true love, whatever their current beef happened to be. News of the world or classical music? Forget it! Duff switched the radio off in disgust, regretting once again that he had not brought any books on tape.

As he approached the last Savannah exit, the old Toyota let out a rebellious cough, then began to buck. Duff looked at the gas gauge in disbelief—empty! How could that be when he had filled up in St. Augustine? He flicked on his turn signal and pulled the car over, sputtering every inch of the way.

Frustrated, Duff gave the steering wheel a slap. "Who would even want you, you old bastard?" he demanded. "You're going to get some unemployed person to work on time? I doubt it! Why do you keep doing this to me?"

The car didn't answer, and resigned to his fate, Duff consulted his cell phone for nearby garages which did repairs, should the car need further work. A tow truck showed up within twenty minutes.

The mechanic's Georgia accent was so thick Duff couldn't understand him, but as the tall, thin copper-headed guy pointed to the trail of oil leading from the interstate to the car itself, he nodded in understanding. Oil leak, sure. Duff climbed into the truck's passenger seat, and responded with what he hoped were appropriate 'yeahs,' 'uhms' and 'you bets' to the young man's incomprehensible run-on chatter.

No more than a quarter of mile or so heading toward the city of Savannah, they pulled into a Texaco service station. It was located right on the edge of a clean, classy-looking shopping center, which hosted a number of upscale, brand-name stores. And across the street from the mall—a beautiful motel with a sign that proclaimed it 'Olde Magnolia.The three-story building was painted pink, very Southern-looking, Spanish moss dripping from the trees around it.

And all of it within walking distance.

Relieved that he would have a more-than-decent place to spend the night, Duff crossed the street, intending to sign in. His spirits lifted even more as he saw the Japanese restaurant, half hidden by several flowering magnolia trees at the side of the motel. Feeling almost fortunate that his car had acted up again, he went to check out the restaurant.

There were Japanese restaurants, and there were Japanese restaurants. This one was called "Hokusai" and that was a good sign. The front doorway was flanked by granite griffins, and as he approached the door, and looked it, he saw that it was indeed an upscale place. It had authentic, but not ostentatious décor. It had prints by Katsushika Hokusai, the Mt. Fuji artist, on the wall. He wondered if all thirty-six views of the famous mountain would be there.

A uniformed man opened the door and made a little bow. "I would invite you in, sir, but we do ask our patrons to dress a bit more formally. "Duff's mouth watered. The aromas coming from the kitchen were divine. "I need to go check in across the street," he said, "but I will change clothes and I definitely be back for dinner."

"Very good," the waiter said, with another courtly bow. "You should reserve a table. We're full up every night."

"I'll do that, then." He stepped inside the restaurant and gave his name to the hostess. She was tiny, sleekly black-haired and beautiful.

"We can have a single at seven. Phone number?" She smiled at him, as no girl had smiled at him in a long time.

He recited his cel number." I'm going across the street to check in there. So if you need to talk to me, call the motel and ask for my room. I'll be back at seven."

Feeling jubilant, Duff crossed the street to The Olde Magnolia, and went into the office.

There were no problems with registering. "We have a room that looks out over the pool," the normal-appearing woman with "Arline' embroidered on her immaculate white blouse told him. "Will that be all right?" She had a sweet Southern accent, which he found charming. In fact, as he looked around the spacious lobby, beautifully furnished with gleaming antiques and bowls of flowers everywhere, he thought that everything about the Olde Magnolia was charming.

"Perfect," he said. "And I'm going to take advantage of that right now."

He loved his room, number 326. Again, it oozed Southern charm. A canopy bed, dripping with white organdy and lace, stood in the center of the room. A Queen Anne desk and chair flanked one wall, and a matching cabinet above it hid the television. In the front of the window overlooking the pool, were two graceful armchairs, covered with blue and gold flowered tapestry, with a small, curve-legged table between them.

The room had a mini-refrigerator stocked with beer, wine and mixers and soda, so he wouldn't even need to leave the room to have a drink. Instead of the usual plastic glasses, two crystal goblets, beautifully patterned in silver, sat on a shelf over the bar.

He was more than pleased about that, as his own crystal had been stolen along with his other belongings.

"Wow, this is so classy!" The registration price had been classy, too, but he deserved one night of luxury, didn't he, after his experience at the Ocean View?

He unpacked his suitcase, hanging his new, used clothing on the hangers provided. He changed into his bathing suit, put the short terry robe on over it, and grabbed the beach towel. On impulse, he took a can of imported beer from the bar-fridge, and headed for the pool.

He hardly dared to believe that everything would go along well without some kind of catastrophe happening.

An intricate, white wrought-iron fence surrounded the pool. It had a swinging gate at each end, while the pool itself ran lengthwise with the building. Duff went in from the back side, and chose a vacant table. Most of the other tables were occupied by good-looking couples, pairs or trios of pretty young girls, a couple of families with children. Everyone was well-behaved, even the young kids, who were splashing in the shallow end of the pool, but not yelling or trying to drown each other, or running around the edge of the pool.

He draped his towel over the back of the chair, and set the beer on the table. He took off his robe and laid it on one of the chairs. He couldn't wait to get in the pool. Not even bothering with the steps at the shallow side; he sat on the side of the deep end and simply let himself fall into the water.

It was exactly the right temperature—warm enough to be comfortable, cool enough to be refreshing. He swam two quick laps the length of the pool, then let himself drift and float, looking up. The intense blue of the sky contrasted with the snowy white clouds thrilled his artistic soul. How beautiful it was, the simplest of sights, and yet, how few people ever really looked at it, and really saw it. That's what he loved about art. If, in his new position at Simon's Rock, he could teach his students to see, to really see past the 'ordinary' of what the world saw, he would consider his work a great success.

He only regretted that his lovely Raina was not there to share this experience with him. He knew she had the sensitivity to learn to appreciate the finer things in life, if only she would let him show her. What he really yearned to share with her was the art of romance. But, was that ever going to happen?

"Oh, Raina," he murmured aloud. "If only you were here with me now."

In total shock, he heard her laughter. And Marisol's. Treading water, he peered the length of the pool—and there they were, heading toward the gate, opposite from the one he had used when he came into the pool. They stopped, discussing something with each other, gesturing at the motel and across the street toward the mall. They turned for a minute, their backs toward him.

Duff took that few seconds to hurl himself out of the pool, heaving himself over the side like a fish flopping onto the surround. He scrambled to his feet, grabbed his robe, the towel and the beer and fled out the back gate. The corridor door was right there, and he made a dash for it, hoping there were enough people on the pool terrace to block their view of him.

He peeked around the door. With relief, he realized they had not noticed him. They opened the front gate and entered the pool area, still laughing. Duff ducked back against the wall, then, dripping, ran up the two flights to his room.

Back in his room, he heaved a grateful sigh. They had not seen him—but what were the chances the three of them would end up at the same motel? Well, he didn't have to worry about calling her tonight. He knew where she was. But it left him with a guilty, uncomfortable feeling. If she ever saw him, she'd be sure he was following her, checking upon her—and lying to her, since he was supposed to be in Maine. She'd never forgive him. Never.

He didn't know what room they had, though. For all he knew, they might be sharing the room next to him, or across the hall. He'd better check.

He picked up the phone and called the desk.

"What room are Raina Hudson and Marisol Martinez in?"

"Room thirty-three on the first floor. Would you like me to connect you?"

"Oh, no! he sputtered. "I just want to pay them a visit later, and I didn't know what room they're in."

"I'll let them know you were asking about them," Arline said.

"No, please don't. I—I want to take them out to dinner, and I want it to be a surprise. I'll call them myself later."

Arline sounded doubtful. "All right, but usually we inform people when someone wants their room number or phone. There are lots of stalkers around, although of course I don't mean you, Mr. Duffy. I could tell you're a gentleman."

"Thanks," he said. "No, you certainly don't have to worry about me."

He replaced the receiver and walked to the window which overlooked the pool. Raina and Marisol had taken over the exact table he had chosen. He drew the drapes together so that no slit of outside showed. He'd have to be mega-careful not to be seen when he went around back to the restaurant.

Duff considered. *Maybe I should leave while they're at the pool and I can get out of here. Oh my God, what if they see my car in the lot! No—my car is at the gas station Maybe I should just order in—pizza or Kentucky fried.* But no—he had paid a good price to stay at this beautiful motel, and he really wanted to try out the Japanese restaurant. He knew Raina would never go there. He flicked the tab on his beer and eased into a chair. *Now, if I only had some crackers and cheese to go with the beer.*

A slight knock sounded on his door. Wondering who in the world that could be at four-thirty in the afternoon, he went to answer it.

A teen-aged boy wearing a starched white shirt, like Arline's, with his name—Steven—embroidered on the pocket, stood there. In his hand he carried a plate with cheese and crackers nicely arranged on the dish, and covered with plastic wrap.

He held it out to Duff. "Compliments of the Olde Magnolia."

Behind him, Duff saw a serving cart with wheels, the kind on which meals are delivered to rooms. It was covered with plates like the one he offered Duff.

Sensing prickles up and down his spine, Duff accepted a plate and thanked Steven. He walked back to the window, picking up one of the crystal goblets on the way, feeling as though he had entered a strange new world, one in which his every wish was immediately answered.

He looked up at the ceiling, and addressed whomever lay beyond it. "Okay. I wish when we get back to the office that Raina accepts my proposal of marriage."

He laughed at himself. Yeah. When pigs fly, as Granny Victoria would say.

He laid the plate on the table, removed the plastic wrap and poured the beer into the goblet. Brie with a red sauce like cranberry, and rice crackers. Perfect. But he couldn't resist taking a peek at Raina. He went to the window and pulled the curtains apart just enough to get a glimpse of her.

He watched her for a few seconds, and his love for her filled him, as it always did when he was near her. Or—when she filled his thoughts and there was no room for anything else. Then guilt-stricken, he dropped the curtain, and sat back in his chair.

Maybe you should let her have her space.

He nearly dropped his glass. Whose voice was that? It must be his imagination—or maybe a guilty conscience. *I love her. I just love to look at her. I never get enough of that.*

Make another wish.

"Okay, then...I wish she would go to Hokusai tonight and learn to love Japanese food." He laughed at himself. "Fat chance of that, Duff. Fat chance."

Give her some space. It will all work out.

Again the strange voice that wasn't a voice, but more of a feeling. But whose non-voice was it, and where did it come from? But the voice's demand was growing on him. He shouldn't be watching her when she didn't know that he was. And he wasn't trying to show up everywhere she and Raina landed, but Fate seemed to be arranging it that way.

Time for dinner. He figured he would be safe if he left the motel by the back door, and hurried around to the rear of the building to Hokusai. He glanced at his watch. If he were going to keep his reservation, it was time to get dressed.

He stripped off the tee and shorts. He selected the Dockers, which didn't look brand new, but were in very good condition, the blue and white striped dress shirt, and the navy blazer. He checked himself in the mirror. He actually looked good, he thought, in his second hand, hastily-purchased cheap clothes. In truth, he realized, he looked better than he usually did in his own clothing.

He felt a shiver of unreality as left the Olde Magnolia by the back door, and with a jolt spied Marisol's red Focus parked in the nearest space. Their room must be in the back. Well, the magnolia trees would hide him once it got a little bit darker, when he had to walk back. It seemed so bizarre that everything was overlapping on this part of the trip. If they discovered him, how on earth could he explain it?

He should leave the motel now, go register at another one. No, this one had put a big dent in his credit card. He would stay the night, leave in the morning as soon as he was sure he was safe from being seen. Tomorrow night would be the third evening. He could call Raina "from Maine" and find out where she was.

But first, a Japanese dinner with sake, a Japanese liquor made from rice, plum wine and chopsticks. He loved eating with chopsticks. He went into the restaurant and checked in with the hostess.

She definitely flirted with him as she pretended for a moment not to be able to find his name, then asked him several times in her lilting accent if he were 'Michael Duffy.'

"I'm Michael Duffy, yes," he said, grinning for the first time that day. He thought her cute as a button, and if he weren't so addicted to Raina...

She flounced her short skirt in front of him, showing off a pair of exquisite legs, as she directed him to his seat. The restaurant, which was large in area, had been proportioned into smaller sections by the use of traditional-looking Japanese screens, beautifully decorated with elegant art and touches of gold or silver. She sat him in a corner, with a screen portraying elegant, long-legged cranes and purple iris, which hid him from the tables in the front part of the restaurant. He liked the privacy. He could see out into the restaurant, but not be easily seen, especially if he sat back closer to the wall.

She handed him the handsome menu, also decorated in Japanese style art and touches of gold. "My name is Kio."

"Kio." He pronounced it as she had: key-oh.

She smiled again and held his eyes. "What you doing after dinner? You want to go clubbing, maybe?"

Astounded, he sat back and stared at her. "What? Who? Me?"

"Yes, you. You handsome, wear good clothes. I like go clubbing with nice American boy sometimes."

"Uh..." He was about to tell her 'no,' but something rang in his brain. Raina had told him he had to have two dates before he asked her out again. Well, this could be one of them...and uhm, Myrtle Simmons the other, maybe?

He smiled back at her. "Yeah, maybe, Kio. Let me think about it."

"Oh-kaaay!" she said, and did a little dance as she glided away.

He opened the menu, his brain whirling. What was happening to him, anyway? This trip was turning out to be something much more than he ever thought it would be, both good and bad. You have to take the good with the bad. That is really such a dumb statement. It's the bad you have to take with the good.

The menu was all in Japanese. Well, that was beyond him. He folded it back together. He'd ask the waiter for a recommendation. All he knew was that he wanted sake, and he would eat the meal with chopsticks.

The waiter brought him the sake in a tiny glass not much bigger than a jigger used to measure hard liquor for mixed drinks.

His English wasn't as clear as Kio's, but Duff didn't have any trouble understanding him "What will you have this evening, sir?"

"What would you recommend?"

The waiter mentioned several dishes, and Duff had no idea what was in any one of them. But, this was turning into an interesting adventure. "Surprise me," Duff said. "Something I wouldn't ordinarily order."

The waiter bowed. "Very good, sir."

Duff sipped his sake.

He looked around at the restaurant, which was quickly filling up. He sat back, feeling relaxed and comfortable. Sure enough, handsomely framed prints of Hokusai's Mt. Fuji prints adorned the walls. He loved this. Why couldn't Raina learn to love this, too?

Oh, Raina, I'm so crazy about you, and this whole situation is so crazy, I just don't know what game Fate is playing here.

Just as he finished the last sip, and set his glass on the table. Kio appeared around the screen, carrying two more small glasses, and a plate of sushi. She set the sake down in front of him, the sushi between them, and slid into the seat opposite.

"My shift over," she said. "I sit with you few minutes, but then I go to office in back. You want go out after you eat?"

Why not?

"Sure. What time?" *It will be good and dark by the time I get back to the motel. Fate working with me, for once.*

She winked. "Does not matter. I do paper work in office back there." She pointed to the back of the restaurant. "We go out that way. But first, enjoy your dinner. When finished, go back there for me."

He looked at the sushi. It was beautifully presented, artistic with a variation of rolled fillings. He picked one up and nibbled at it. "Delicious!"

She smiled. "Everything delicious here. We five-star."

"I can believe that. Thank you. Where are you from, Kio?"

Her eyes twinkled. "Japan."

He laughed. "I know that. What city or town."

"Nara. Very old town. You know Nara?"

He shook his head. "No, I just know the big cities, Tokyo, Kyoto..." He was about to add Hiroshima and Nagasaki, but decided against it. Why bring that up and possibly dampen such an exciting evening?

"They make Hollywood film in Nara," she said. "*Last Samurai.* You know it?"

"Yes," he said, surprised. "I love that movie."

"I love, too." She regarded him over the rim of her sake glass, slanted black eyes sparkling, her shiny, straight black hair framing her exquisite face. Duff thought she looked like a sleek black panther—but a friendly one.

Time flew while they made small talk, sipped their drinks and finished off the sushi. The waiter arrived with Duff's dinner, plus a plethora of side dishes, steaming white rice, egg rolls, several sauces for his entrée.

He didn't know what the entrée was, and he didn't care.

He thought he had never been so hungry. He could hardly wait to dive in.

Kio stood and looked down at him, although she was so small she didn't have far to look. "Okay, take time, but come back, get me when done." She gestured toward the door in the back again, then left, silent as a shadow.

Duff positioned the chopsticks and took the first bite of his entrée, and sighed with pleasure. Life could only get any better if Raina were sitting next to him. *Oh, Raina, I so wish you were here.*

Twenty-three

He heard the new hostess seating customers on the other side of the screen, heard their chairs scraping on the floor as they sat. "The waiter will be right with you," she said, and glided away.

"I know I'm going to hate this," he heard Raina say.

He jumped, then froze, and one of his chopsticks nearly fell out of his hand. He fumbled and caught it just before it clicked onto the table.

No! This could not be happening!

"Just give it a chance," Marisol said.

"Do we have to eat sushi? Raw fish—yuk. What kind of people eat raw fish?"

"Let's give it a try. All kinds of people eat all kinds of things. Americans aren't always right about everything, you know. Let's live a little."

"I know you're just trying to get me to like what Duff likes. Why can't he like what I like?"

He heard Marisol give a patient sigh. "Because he's better educated and has had more experiences in life than you have had, and a broader exposure to a lot of things. You could grow with him, Raina, and that's a good thing to have that chance. You don't need to sit in that office year after year, getting nowhere. You have an opportunity for a great life."

Duff felt his insides turn to jelly as he listened to Marisol and his eyes began to moist over with emotion. Marisol—he'd never known she felt that way, or had been trying to convince Raina of his merits. She had told him she was going to talk to Raina, but he thought just general things—nice guy, good future, and so forth. He was overcome with gratitude. If he ever had a chance to thank her, well, he didn't know how he would, but he would try.

Raina's voice held a plaintive note. "How do you know I'll never get anywhere in that office? I could be assistant office manager, or even office manager, if Dianne—"

"Ha!" Marisol snorted. "Why do you think you're not already assistant office manager, with a raise and more authority, and all that?"

"I already know the procedures better than anyone else, and I help anyone who asks me to. Dianne knows that."

"Yes, she knows it, and so does everyone else. But—how old is Dianne? Forty, forty-one? She had her kids young, and they're almost grown and out of the house. She's not going to share anything with you, Raina, because she wants all the power, all the prestige, and everything else for herself."

Duff sat, spellbound. He had thought the same thing himself, but when he said anything to Raina, she had brushed it off. He'd only been there six months; he didn't know how the office politics worked, and he was too hard on Dianne, she'd said.

Now, here was Marisol's confirmation. Raina was too good to spend her life in that office under Dictator Dianne's thumb. Raina was smart, Raina was capable, Raina could run the place as well as Dianne could, but she would never get the chance.

Duff wanted to get up, run around the screen and kiss Marisol.

The waiter approached them, and asked what they wanted to drink.

"Sake," Marisol said. "And with the dinner we'll have plum wine."

"The plum wine sounds good," Raina commented, her voice lifting.

"It is superb," the waiter said. "And the menu is in Japanese, so if you'd like some suggestions for dinner, I'll be glad to help you."

Raina's voice again. "I just don't want to eat eel or whale or squid, or any of those squirmy things. Can I get something made with chicken or beef?"

"Certainly." Duff envisioned his little bow.

"And I'll take a fish dish," Marisol said.

The waiter ran through an impressive list of fish, and she chose one.

"Chopsticks?"

"No!" Raina said at the same time Marisol said "Yes."

"Oh, give it a try," Marisol urged.

Duff began to pick silently at his food.

The waiter came to check on him.

"Is everything all right, sir?"

He nodded. He couldn't speak and let Raina and Marisol know he was there, although there was so much giggling on the other side of the screen, they probably wouldn't hear him anyway.

"Would you like more sake, or some plum wine?"

He shook his head again.

The waiter wrinkled his forehead. "Which one would you not like?"

Duff shrugged and made waving motions with both hands.

"Is there a problem, sir? Would you like to speak to the manager?"

Duff formed 'no' with his mouth, and again shook his head.

The waiter stared at him for a long moment. "Then I'll bring your check."

Duff nodded, and when the waiter returned, turned over his credit card without even looking at the amount. He signed and added a twenty-dollar tip. The meal had been worth it.

"Thank you." The waiter bowed, and stood aside, expecting dollar to precede him and head for the front of the restaurant.

Duff backed away, keeping the screen between him and the table on the other side of the screen. The waiter began to protest, but Duff rolled his eyes and put his finger to his lips. He pointed to the back door, and slid along the side of the wall as he aimed toward it. The waiter watched, bewildered. Duff reached the door, tapped on it lightly, and without being invited, opened it and went into the back room.

It was an office, with desks and computers, file cabinets and a copying machine. Kio looked up as he came in and favored him with a broad smile. "Ah, here you are. I am ready."

She had changed out of her hostess uniform. She wore a silky gray dress, very short, with no back and a plunging front. Duff attempted to remain cool, but felt as though his eyes were bugging out of his head. She was curvy, but very small, so nothing really bulged out of place. Exquisite. *It's just that she looked as if she were barely wearing anything. This should satisfy Raina all right! Well, this and Myrtle Simmons—I've fulfilled my two dates with other women.*

She took his arm, and started toward the exit. "We take my car, come on."

Of course she had a Toyota, a nice one, white with a sunroof. She clicked the doors open and motioned for him to walk around to the other side.

He climbed in and fastened his seat belt. "Where are we going?"

"Dominico's. You ever been there?"

"No, I'm not from here. I'm just passing through."

"That why I ask you out. No strings, you know?"

Yes, he did know. But she was adorable. *Why wouldn't she want to meet someone she could have a relationship with? Well that was for her to know, and for him not to worry about.*

They headed toward the city, and he noted that she was a careful driver, not speeding, not inconsiderate, not running yellow lights to save a few seconds. Duff always felt like yelling out the window at drivers who did that, "What are you going to do with the ten seconds you saved?" But he never did. There were a few rude replies he could think of, but it really wasn't worth the hassle.

Dominico's sat on the corner of a busy road, and the parking lot was already full when Kio pulled in. Duff could hear the music, fast and loud with a compelling beat. His foot began tapping all by itself.

She glanced at him as she circled the lot, looking for a space. "You dance?"

"I have a feeling I'm going to tonight!"

Maybe it was the sake, maybe it was the magic of the evening, maybe it was being somewhere he didn't have to be Michael Duffy, prospective art professor, and maybe it was Kio herself—but Duff fell into the mood of the club with no problem at all. He let himself go, danced with Kio, let the rhythm of the music fill him and guide his movements. Sometimes he found himself dancing with other women, but Kio always came back, laughing at him, handing him another glass of wine.

Finally, still smiling, Kio said, "Michael Duffy, we go now."

"Why? I'm having fun."

"It two o'clock. Must go work tomorrow. You need to sleep now."

Suddenly he realized he did feel tired. His legs trembled as if made of plastic.

She laughed at him. "You had good time. Me, too. I not forget you."

He fought an urge to grab her and kiss her. He looked at her, but Raina's face rose up in his mind. No, he told himself. There is fun, and there is love, and tonight was not about love. It was about my second date and fun, and that's all.

They drove back toward the mall and the Olde Magnolia. "I drop you here," she said as she turned into the motel.

"Sounds good to me," he muttered, wanting only to fall into his canopy bed.

She smiled again, as she unlocked his door from her control panel. "You handsome, you know, Michael Duffy. Girl is lucky."

He gazed at her, surprised by her remark. "What makes you think I have a girlfriend?"

She giggled. "Because you no come on to me." She gave his shoulder a slight push with her tiny hand.. "Good night, Michael Duffy. I had good time with you."

He fought his way upstairs, clutching the bannister and trying to remember what floor he was on, and his room number. Was it 325? He tried his key card, but it didn't flash green, didn't open the door. He tried the next door, 327. No luck there, either.

Suddenly the door to 325 flew open. An elderly man with disheveled white hair sticking up all over his head glanced at Duff, then up and down the hall. "What the hell's going on here?"

"Sorry," Duff blurted, staggering to the other side of the hall. Maybe his room was there. Yeah, 326, that was it. The door opened, and he fell inside the room, dragging the door shut behind him.

He stumbled across the room, peeled off his clothes, and with some effort managed to hang them up, although he couldn't seem to get the blue blazer to stay on the hanger. Finally, it cooperated, and he turned toward the bed. Pajamas—? He couldn't remember where they were. His boxers would have to do.

As he headed toward the bed, he heard something from the pool area. He went to the window, drew the drapes, and looked down.

The lights ringing the pool illuminated the scene below. There, at two-thirty in the morning, were Raina and Marisol splashing in the pool. He heard their laughter. He watched for a moment, feeling his love for Raina rise again, and the longing for her swept over him.

He let out a long sigh as he gazed down at her. "Oh, Raina. How crazy is this? We had a Japanese dinner together tonight, and you never even knew it."

Allow her her privacy, Duff! That danged inner voice, and he knew it was right. He drew the curtain closed. He fell into bed, hugging Sleeping Beauty close to him.

Twenty-four

Duff's room phone rang, waking him. Groaning, he turned over and reached for it.

He heard Arline's voice. "Mr. Duffy, it's after eleven, which is check-out time. We need to know whether you're leaving Olde Magnolia this morning, or if you wish to stay another day. If you opt to stay with us another day and night, we can automatically put it on your credit card for you."

"Another day," he managed to gasp, and fumbled trying to replace the receiver. After the third or fourth try, he got it in the right place. He spread-eagled on his back, staring up into the white lace of the canopy, wondering what the heck he had done to get to feel so awful. Everything ached as if he'd been on a ten-mile hike over rugged terrain. His head ached, and his mouth felt dry as the desert.

Oh, yes. The Japanese restaurant, Kio and Dominico's. He remembered now.

He heard himself groan again. *What was I thinking?*

No matter how he tried, he couldn't get back to sleep. An hour later he sat up and reached for the phone again. He dialed the office.

"Yes. Mr. Duffy?"

"Room service, please."

She transferred him to the kitchen.

"Six cups of black coffee, please, soon as possible."

"Six cups?"

"Yes. Hurry, please."

"Ten minutes, sir."

Ten minutes. That left time for a shower, if he could find the bathroom. He got up and turned around several times, trying to orient himself. Oh, yes, there was the bathroom, to the right, just where it had been yesterday.

He turned on the shower water as hot as he could stand it. It felt wonderful coursing over his body, but it didn't do much for the desert in his mouth or the cotton in his head. Abruptly, he turned the shower to cold.

"Eiehhhhhhh!" He squealed like a stuck calf. That was more brutal than he'd expected, but it did do the job of waking him up. Shivering, he turned it back to warm.

When his body felt comfortable again, he repeated the cold and hot cycle.

He hurried to throw on shorts and a shirt, and the expected knock at the door came just as he pulled up his pants.

"Here you are, sir. Six cups." The messenger looked around the motel rooms as if expecting five other people. With a puzzled look, he placed the tray on the desk. Duff handed him a five dollar bill and closed the door behind him.

He carried the tray over to the table by the window, and sat in one of the armchairs. His coffee had been delivered in ivory-colored ceramic mugs, showing a magnolia tree and the motel's scripted logo. As he picked up one of the mugs, he glanced down at the pool. Several people lay in the lounge chairs, another couple sat at a table drinking coffee, and three children splashed in the pool. Now that he had regained his senses, he heard their joyous sing-song refrain—Marco Polo! Marco Polo!

One by one, he drained the mugs of the steaming black liquid.

"I wonder what Raina and Marisol are going to do today?" He wished with all his heart that they would spend the day around the pool, so he could sit in his room and do nothing. But he had a feeling that was not to be. And, he remembered, he had to go across the street and fetch the Toyota.

"With the way things have been going on this trip, someone will have stolen my car." That grim thought got him going. He'd better go get his vehicle, and also check to see whether the red Focus was in the lot.

He could ask at the desk if the girls had checked out. But, no, that would seem suspicious. If he were the good friend he'd claimed to be, wouldn't he know if they had gone?

He longed to call Raina, but she had given him a three-day ultimatum, and he still had a day to wait. In the meantime, he had better buff up his Maine story, so he knew what he was talking about, and therefore sound more credible.

He made it across the busy, four-lane highway without incident, and there was the car waiting for him.

He briefly thought about popping in just to say hello to Kio, but decided against it. No, that was a one-night adventure, and even if she were willing, he didn't want a second-night adventure. Not after the way he felt today.

Back at the Olde Magnolia, he circled the lot looking for Marisol's car. He didn't see it. He went around again, more slowly. Nope, no red Focus. He parked his car in the rear of the lot where it was half-hidden by the dark shadow of a looming tree, and went back up to his room, trying to decide what to do.

~ * ~

Raina leafed through the folders she had picked up from the showcase in the motel lobby. She picked up one and waved it at her friend. "Hey, Marisol, want to take the Haunted Ghost Tour? It says here Savannah is the most haunted city in the United States."

Marisol flopped on her bed on her stomach, her feet in the air, and glanced over at her. "Well, I was hoping you'd be up for some of the historic sites... Sherman's headquarters, or the Heritage Museum."

She felt a flicker of annoyance. "Oh, I leave all that history stuff to Duff. No, I want to do something fun, not wander around through moldering buildings, hearing about all the stuff that was. I'm a here and now person."

Marisol laughed. "I've noticed. Okay, I'm up for ghosts and goblins. Let's grab breakfast, then ask about it at the desk."

The Olde Magnolia provided a sumptuous breakfast, with omelets made to order if anyone wanted one, and yummy things to go into them: onions, mushrooms, asparagus tips, avocado slices , several kinds of cheese.

Marisol finished off her mushroom, crabmeat creation, and pushed the plate away.

"Raina, I want to ask you something. Seriously."

"About the ghost tour? I thought I filled you in on that. Here, look at the folder yourself."

Marisol laughed. "No, not about that. About Duff."

"I've told you a hundred times how I feel about Duff." Slightly annoyed, Raina gazed at Marisol. Why did she keep insisting on discussing this? "I like him, I respect him, and I am actually physically attracted to him, but I don't think I love him. And I feel so sorry for him about that, and all he's going through with the death of his grandmother. I hope he's not too depressed when we get back to the office."

Marisol leaned forward, her elbows on the table. "Raina, you do know how much he loves you, don't you?"

Why was Marisol insisting on this discussion? Raina tossed back her hair. "Well, I'd have to be deaf and blind not to!"

Marisol fixed her with a long look. "So what are you going to do about it, other than feel sorry for him? That's not what he wants."

Her cup of coffee suddenly seemed to get very interesting to Raina, as she searched its dark depths, and didn't reply.

"Raina?"

After a long moment, she looked up and shrugged. "I just don't know. You can't imagine how I agonize about this. I've thought a lot about what you said the other day, how I could have a better life."

"And?"

"I don't know if I want a better life. I like my life as it is."

"So you wouldn't miss Duff at all if he went away?"

"I suppose I would, in a way, but I don't think I want to marry him, and it seems like that's what he's got on his mind. As soon as his college job comes through, he'll want to whisk me away to some other part of the country—"

"And what's wrong with that? Thousands of wives move with their husbands when a new job or a promotion comes along."

Raina sighed. "He's just not fun, Marisol. When we go out, he seems so uptight, and he's forever explaining things to me, like I'm a child."

"He wants you to have to knowledge to enjoy things, Raina. If you know something about a subject, say Vincent Van Gogh, you get a lot more out of looking at his paintings." She paused and looked down at the table. "I'd give anything to have someone like Duff crazy about me, and just waiting for a chance to give me a new, adventuresome life like Duff is offering you."

"But when I went out with Jake, before Duff came on the scene, our dates were fun."

Marisol threw up her hands in exasperation. "Raina! Jake worked at the car wash for minimum wage. He called awnings 'yawnings.' There was no future there for a smart, pretty girl like you."

Raina twisted the emerald ring on her little finger, and didn't answer. She felt pressured, and she didn't like pressure. Maybe that was why she had never insisted that Dianne give her more responsibility at the office. She didn't like to pressure others, either.

Marisol looked very serious. "Raina, don't get mad at me, please, but I'm going to be very honest with you. You need to grow up and think about your future."

Raina felt defensive. "How can you say that to me? What about you? What about your future?"

"It's not the same. I'm part of the Latino community at home, expected to marry a Latino and have Latino kids. Our families are joined at the hip, and I don't have the freedom to go off and have a new life. Also, I'm not as smart as you are. If you married Duff, I bet he would want you take college courses and get your degree."

Raina ignored the last part of her sentence. "Why do you think I'm so much smarter than you are? We essentially do the same work."

Marisol shook her head. "You run the office, Raina. You don't know it, but Dianne sure does. Why do you think every time someone goes to her with a question, she says, 'See Raina about it. I don't have time for that now.' Why do you think I'm in your cubicle every morning, going over what I have to do for the day?"

Raina stared at her, speechless. About all she could manage was, "Really?"

"Yes, really. That's what I mean about growing up. You're way too smart and capable for the job you're doing, Raina, without chance of recognition or advancement, because Lady Dianne will never get off her throne. If you gave Duff a real chance, and tried to learn from him, you could grow so much. You could be someone special." She winked. "More special, I mean."

Confused and embarrassed, Raina pushed her best friend's remarks aside. "I don't want to think about that now. Let's go find out about the Haunted Tour."

They stood and Marisol grabbed Raina's arm. "Promise me you'll think about what I said."

"I will. But right now, let's just go have fun."

Marisol sighed. "Okay, fun it is."

Twenty-five

When the room phone rang, it was the mechanic from the gas station. Duff couldn't understand his thick Georgia accent, but somewhere in there he picked out the name of the service station. Perfect. It was a good time to leave the motel.

The girls were in the pool again. Duff pulled the curtain back just enough to ascertain it really was Raina and Marisol laughing and splashing around down there, then resolutely drew it closed. He would leave the Olde Magnolia now, when he was sure they wouldn't be headed out on the road again. He would get enough of a head start to make very sure he didn't end up at the same place again.

He circled around the motel on the opposite side from the pool, and passed the red Focus. He couldn't help himself. Sidling up to the car, he wet his finger and drew three hearts on the windshield. They'd dry off, and Raina would never see them and know he'd been there, but he had the satisfaction of knowing he'd done it.

"Excuse me, sir, what are you doing?"

Duff looked up in alarm and saw a uniformed attendant starting at him.

Caught doing something stupid again. Dumb! Dumb! Dumb!

He stepped away from the car, and threw the man a sidewise look. "Oh, I just love red Ford Focuses. Just can't resist them. Can't wait 'til I can afford one."

The attendant nodded slowly. "Sort of a fetish thing, right?"

Duff suppressed his desire to laugh, and nodded.

The green-clad man inched closer. He looked around as if trying to see if anyone could hear. In a loud whisper, he confided, "I've got sort of a fetish of my own—turtles. I just love 'em, can't get enough of them." He regarded Duff with a conspiratorial look. "I don't tell everybody this, you know, but you seem like you'd understand. They're so hard and soft all at once, y'know, and those little snaky heads and those adorable tails..."

"Oh, yeah, absolutely," Duff agreed as he backed away. "But I gotta go now. Nice to talk to you. Bye." He strode off toward the highway as fast as he could go.

He was never so glad to see the old black Toyota. It seemed like a long-lost friend.

He drove back to Interstate 95, and turned north, He couldn't wait, gathered up his courage and called Raina. How he wanted to tell her about the guy with the turtle fetish—he could have met that guy in Maine, right?"

"We're leaving our motel in about an hour," she told him. "Don't know exactly where we're going."

"You stop early, about four o'clock," he'd told her. "Get off the highway and check in somewhere."

"We will."

"Be sure the motel's in a well-lighted area, and—"

"Duff!"

She'd clicked off in annoyance. "Whoops, I went too far," he told the car. "I have to stop telling her what to do, but it's so hard." He thought a moment. "And I didn't get the chance to tell her I've had two dates." He contemplated a little longer, wondering what he could tell her. Then he knew. He wouldn't mention Myrtle Simmons or Kio, not until a few years from now when he could confess everything and they've have a good laugh. But he did know with certainty who the two dates would be with. Or maybe just one, long enough to say goodbye. Tanya.

He turned on the radio. More of what he'd been offered in northern Florida and Georgia; nothing he really wanted to hear. Why couldn't he remember to pick up a book on tape? He'd be sure to do that when he stopped for dinner.

He'd checked the map, and estimated it would take about three hours to drive through South Carolina before hitting the next state border. He and they would have to stop for the night. He drummed his fingers on the steering wheel as he drove. There was nothing to do but drive, or talk to himself, or sing to himself.

How about some of those old hymns he had loved from the old days, when he'd gone to church?

Humming "The Old Rugged Cross," and as the words and melody came back to him, he lost himself in the majesty of the hymn, and let himself sing it with gusto. When he'd sung that several times, he followed it with "Holy, Holy, Holy," which had been a particular favorite of his, then with fragments of anything else he could remember, including "Rudolph, the Red-Nosed Reindeer," which he couldn't quite get out of his head. He managed to keep himself so engrossed trying to remember the words that he didn't notice the gas gauge until the red light flickered on and caught his attention.

Knowing it could be quite a way before the next exit, he swerved off to the left and drove into the first available station. He'd been testing his vocal chords on "Will the Circle be Unbroken?" which had been the one his grandmother had loved, and he continued humming it absent-mindedly as he put his charge card into the slot and filled his tank. Once in a while, he caught himself singing, and looked around, hoping no one had been listening.

The gas station complex included Clem's truck stop, a large diner that catered to truckers and carried lots of merchandise that those doing heavy-duty driving might need or desire. "I wonder if I could get some books on tape there," he wondered aloud. He parked the car and went in to investigate. He wandered the aisles of the store, humming, and fascinated by the assortment of merchandise and corny souvenirs.

There was a battery for everything under the sun, it seemed, and piles of rope, cords and electrical attachment for every possible use. There were racks of heavy work shoes and boots—from long rubber hip-length boots, to the pull-on kind of galoshes he'd worn as a kid, and cowboy boots. He picked up a pair of brownish-green boots that looked as though they might be made of alligator skin, or lizard. Hmm—how would he look in a pair of these boots? Where could he wear them? Would Raina like them or would she think he was stranger than ever? "And He walks with me, and He talks with me..." Probably the boots triggered his subconscious, as he began to hum "In the Garden" again. Then, not thinking of where he was, broke into full song.

By the time he reached the second verse, he heard another voice join in, then a third and a fourth. He wheeled around, and saw a crowd of ten or twelve people, all of whom began to clap along in rhythm as they sang along with him.

"Don't stop!" yelled a woman in jeans and a yellow tee-shirt. She was way overweight, and her dyed, bright yellow hair was tied back in a ponytail.

Duff, embarrassed to the bone, wanted to run, but the crowd surrounded him, all of them singing and urging him on.

He gave in and let go with his very acceptable tenor.

When they finished, his audience applauded.

Several more people, hearing something going on, wandered over.

"Do you know "Will the Circle Be Unbroken?" asked Mrs. Yellow tee-shirt.

"Well, yes, but..."

"Then sing it!" shouted a man in a red lumberjack shirt from the back. Duff looked at him, wondering fleetingly if the rough-looking man with the scraggly beard would beat him up if he refused.

Duff wanted to protest, wanted to leave the store, but something else touched him as he stood there. His grandmother Victoria had loved that song, and he had heard her singing it so many times as she went around doing household things, or cooking, or mending. She had taught him the words, and as a very young boy, before he got too old for such corny things, he sang it with her. And this was just too weird—here, in a truck stop in rural South Carolina, a group of people he didn't even know wanted to sing her favorite hymn with him. It was as if she had requested it in person, and he couldn't refuse.

"Okay." He began the song, and as the crowd joined in, he waved the boot like a baton. When he didn't remember a phrase, someone else did, and when they finished, several women were crying, and Mr. Lumberjack wiped his eyes.

This time there was only silence, sort of a reverent silence, then people began to drift away.

A teen-aged girl lingered, then approached him. "Thank you," she whispered. That was my grandmother's favorite hymn."

"Mine too," he told her. Then following some inner impulse, he asked her, "What was your grandmother's name?"

She smiled "Victoria."

He nodded. Somehow, he'd known she'd say that. "Mine, too."

Suddenly he missed her with all his heart, and was glad that after he did whatever he had to do in Maine, he'd have a few days in Stockbridge to see her again.

As he looked over the books on tape, he knew he'd never forget that moment. He didn't believe in ghosts, or angels, and he wasn't so sure about life after death either, but just then he felt his grandmother's presence as strongly as if she were actually standing next to him.

I'm here, Michael. Sing "Will the Circle Be Unbroken" with me, just one last time.

Twenty-six

"We're almost out of gas," Raina said, peeking past Marisol at the gas tank. "Don't you think we should stop and fill up?"

"Yeah, thanks for reminding me. I was off somewhere, daydreaming."

Raina looked around as Marisol made a sudden swerve into a seedy-looking station. "This is a truck stop!" she said. "Can't we wait 'til the next exit and go someplace where we can get a frozen yogurt or something?"

Marisol shook her head. "I don't know how far the next exit is, and I did let this get too low. If we run out of gas on the interstate, it'll be worse than this truck stop."

Raina nodded. She had a point. She didn't want to be sitting gasless on the shoulder of Interstate 95 either.

Marisol pointed to the truck stop diner. "They'll probably have something to snack on over there at Clem's. It'll be good to get out and stretch our legs anyway." She grinned at her friend. "Maybe something interesting like ox-tails or pigs' feet."

Raina made a face of disgust and added, "You can get some rough characters in those places, though."

Marison smiled at her. "You can get rough people everywhere."

Marisol filled the tank, then parked the car as close to the entrance of the diner as possible, to allay Raina's fears of being attacked getting in or out of the car, and went into the truck stop store.

As they entered the store, an obese woman in jeans and tee-shirt held the door for them. She grinned at them. "You should have been here fifteen minutes ago," she said. "The most wonderful thing just happened here. A spiritual experience. Too bad you missed it." She went out, humming a tune which Raina didn't find familiar.

She gave Marisol a poke in the ribs. "Did you hear that? There was a 'spiritual experience' in here." She giggled. "If we'd been fifteen minutes earlier..."

They moved through the aisles alternately remarking on and trying not to laugh at some of the things they saw. Marisol stopped in front of a display of key chains. "Want to get Michael a souvenir?"

Raina looked at the rack, and started to laugh. "He'd just love something from here, wouldn't he?"

Each key chain had a heavy metal piece at one end, with a colored picture of Clem's on it. Below it was the space for the individual names, written in red enamel script.

"His name has got to be here," Raina said, as she turned the rack, looking for it. She found it, Michael, without any trouble. "I think I will," she said. "It won't mean anything to him, but it'll be funny. We'll tell him it came from 'a spiritual place.'"

Marisol held up another one. "Well, what do you know? Here's Dianne, spelled with the two n's the way she spells it. Should we get her one, too?"

Raina laughed. "Why not? Or do you think she'd like one of those cheap, monogrammed wine glasses better?"

Marisol joined her to look at the plastic goblets, decorated with yellow, trumpet-like flowers, and South Carolina in fancy script. She turned the glass in her hand. "What kind of flower do you think this is?"

Raina shrugged. "I have no idea."

A burly man in a red plaid shirt heard her as he lumbered by, and turned back.

"It's a yellow Jessamine," he said, smiling and showing a couple of bare spaces where he had lost teeth. "State flower of Dixie."

Raina shrunk back against the counter. This was exactly the kind of rough guy she didn't want to run into. "Thanks," she managed to croak.

A pretty girl in her late teens caught up with him. "Oh, there you are, Dad. Sorry I took so long. Wasn't that just amazing? I don't think I'll ever forget it."

He put his arm around her, and Raina relaxed. He looked scary, but if he were this innocent-looking girl's father, he must be okay.

Marisol gave them a long look. "What was amazing—or is it something private? Sorry if I'm not minding my own business, but the lady who just left the store said sort of the same thing."

He seemed happy to answer her question. "It was some young guy who came in here just a few minutes ago." He stretched his hand over his head. "Tall, good-lookin'—he was over there lookin' at the cowboy boots. He just started singin'—coupla hymns we all knew, and pretty soon there was a crowd over there and we all sang. It was just like church, but better." He seemed to stop and think a moment. "There was a real special feeling to it all, the way it just happened."

"Oh," Raina and Marisol said together.

"Listen," the girl said, excitement in her voice, "I recorded it on my phone." She whipped a neon blue cell phone out of her jeans pocket, pressed an assortment of buttons, and held it up. "Can you hear that all right?"

They nodded, as they listened to someone with a haunting tenor voice lead the crowd in singing a plaintive hymn with a catchy rhythm.

Raina was moved in spite of herself, and felt tears spring to her eyes. "That's awesome. He just started singing and everyone else joined in?"

The older man nodded. "It was just a beautiful moment. All these people who didn't know each other all singin' along together with that young bloke. I don't think I ever felt closer to God in church. God bless 'im, whoever he was."

When the couple had gone on down the aisle, Marisol said, "That was awesome. I wish we'd been a few minutes earlier." She shot a sidewise look at her friend. "Say, Raina, did you ever hear Duff sort of humming around the office?"

"Yeah, so what?"

"My cubicle is closer to his than yours. Sometimes he sings in a very low voice—and, well, he has a beautiful tenor voice just like that."

Raina broke into laughter. "Oh, now you're saying that was Duff! You're really trying too hard, Mare."

"Yeah, that's ridiculous, isn't it," Marisol said, nodding her head. "Let's get the key chain for Duff and one of these glasses for Dianne, and get back on the road."

"Suits me fine. You know we'll find Dianne's glass in the trash by the end of the day we give it to her, and maybe Duff's key chain, too. He likes nice things. This is probably a total waste of money."

"I just want Dianne not to be able to say we didn't get her anything." Marisol picked up one of the glasses. "As for Duff, if you give it to him, he'll treasure it the rest of his life."

Raina held up the key chain, looked at it and laughed. "I doubt that."

~ * ~

Raina stared out the window, and couldn't stop thinking about Duff. She turned her head and looked at Marisol, who also seemed lost in her thoughts. "You know, I feel almost guilty. Here we are having such a good time—and poor Duff has had to deal with a funeral. And you know Dianne is going to count this as part of his vacation time. She's just that petty."

"He hasn't worked there long enough to get vacation time," Marisol pointed out. She looked straight ahead, but the question was for Raina. "What are you going to do when his college position comes through and he leaves?"

"What do you mean, what am I going to do?"

"Are you going to go with him?"

"He hasn't asked me."

"He will."

Raina went back to staring out the window. *What am I going to do? If he proposes, what am I going to say? I don't love him—I don't think. But how would I feel if he's not around?* A shaft of something like pain shot through her as she pictured the office without Duff. Michael Duffy. Yes, she had made fun of him, pretended to accept dates with him because she didn't want to hurt his feelings, gone back and complained to Marisol about all the cultural things he was 'forcing' on her, like the art exhibits, the concerts, the plays, the ballet. She would never do those things on her own. She didn't like the French food, she told Marisol; she didn't like the Greek food. Why couldn't he just take her to McDonald's or Kentucky Fried and be done with it? But he had enjoyed the Japanese restaurant experience, and she had even told Marisol about the Hokusai prints on the walls. Maybe she could learn to enjoy a different kind of life. Just maybe. She wasn't all that convinced yet.

Marisol interrupted her thoughts. "Why so quiet?"

She didn't want to get into this with Marisol again. Or did she? She turned her head and looked at her friend. "I'm trying to be honest with myself, maybe for the first time."

"About what?"

"About Duff. Maybe I feel more for him that I've admitted to myself."

"Go on. What are you thinking, or what's more important, what are you feeling?"

"That maybe I've been doing too much negative thinking, not enough positive thinking, and not enough feeling."

"Okay, that's a good start. What about your feelings?"

Raina attempted a laugh, which fell flat. "Hey, are you my therapist now?"

"I will be if it gets you to look below the surface of what you think, for a change."

"I've been thinking about the things you've been saying to me. Duff is a great guy... he does have a bright future. Married to a college professor? I never let myself think about a future like that. Maybe I've just been scared that I'm not up to what he would expect of a wife."

Marisol shook her head. "I don't understand what you're afraid of. You have unlimited potential."

"He's so educated, so intelligent."

"You could learn. You could go to school part time, or nights, or by internet. You have incredible potential, Raina. Everybody sees it but you."

"I guess so. But do I want to do that?"

Marisol took her eyes off the road long enough to give Raina a direct, serious look. "Ten years from now, do you want to be working in that office, putting up with the crap Dianne hands out, begging for raises you know you earned years ago, still eating at fast food places and seeing B movies? Duff has given you a taste of something else, a chance to grow and experience life on a different level. You're nuts if you pass that up."

Raina said in a small voice. "I don't know. I just don't know."

They drove in silence for a while. Finally Marisol said, 'It's four o'clock, There's a place about twenty miles from here called South of the Border. It's really touristy, and has some tacky shops, but I hear the motel is pretty nice, and there are places to eat there, too, the kind you like with tacos, hamburgers, and so on. What do you say? Are you up for that?"

"Yeah, I'm ready to call it a day as far as driving goes. I'm ready for a shower and a dip in the pool, if there is one, and a few tacky souvenir shops, and some fast food. That's what Raina Hudson, the girl who doesn't know what she wants, is ready for right now."

Marisol tossed her a smile. "You're on the verge, kiddo, and I have total faith that you're going to make the right decisions."

Twenty-seven

Duff drove absently along the interstate listening to a James Patterson book on tape that he had bought at the truck stop. It was the perfect thing to listen to while driving. There was an engrossing plot, but no technical details that forced him to concentrate in order to understand the story.

Just before four o'clock, he decided he should look for a motel. He would call Raina as soon as he was settled in somewhere, and find out where they were. His eyes darted to a billboard up ahead. South of the Border. He laughed out loud. "That's too tacky even for Raina and Marisol. But we stopped there once when I was a kid, about six years old, so might as well rev up some memories." He remembered that he was the one who wanted to stop there, and his parents had made fun of the huge cartoony statue with serape and the sombrero that stood outside the complex.

"Oh, let's stop here if he wants to," Granny Gray had said, laughing. Yep, he'd be safe, stopping here.

He slowed down as the approached the exit, took it and drove into the enclave of buildings, stores and amusement rides. He found it all hilarious, as he drove through carefully checking for the red Focus, just in case. Nope, it wasn't there.

He parked his car at the very end of the lot wedged in behind two huge semis—just in case, and went inside the motel to look it over. It was attractive and clean, and surprisingly inexpensive. He went out and looked at the pool, which was right up front. It, too, beckoned, and he would like nothing better than a refreshing dip in the water.

He bought several newspapers from the coin machines in the lobby, checked into his convenient-to-the-pool first floor room, threw his suitcase on the bed and instructed Esbee to take care of it. He took a quick shower to get rid of the dust of the road, then pulled on his swim shorts and grabbed a towel from the rack in the bathroom. Opened the door and stepped out into the hall.

And there was Raina. And Marisol. Checking in.

He paused, one leg in the air, like a pole vaulter frozen in motion. She wore black shorts and a black and white striped tee that stopped above her waist, showing a few inches of tanned skin. Her honey-colored hair bounced over her shoulders as she walked into the office with Marisol. His heart beat faster at the sight of her, and his feelings filled him with warmth. He flashed back to when he had first seen Tanya. Had there been a first time, or had he always known her? That relationship had begun in high school, and they simply carried on. After a while, her parents and his simply expected it would continue.

And maybe it would have, if he hadn't met Raina Hudson. Even when he thought of Tanya now and tried to picture her face, it didn't bring the same rush of feeling.

He ducked back into his room. "Maybe," he said aloud, "Now that I know where they are, I should go get a motel down the road a bit, so I can hang around the pool. Also, I'd like to eat something besides tacos tonight."

He phoned the desk, but the motel clerk wasn't so obliging. "You've just checked in, sir, and given us your credit card. Now you want to leave? Why?"

"Uh...I don't like the room. It's too small for what I want to do."

Bad answer, he knew it the minute he said it.

The clerk's voice was cool. "And what is it you want to do, Mr. Duffy?"

"Uh, never mind that." He decided to tell the truth, sort of. "Someone I don't want to run into just registered here, too. I need to stay somewhere else."

A snort and a short silence. "Can't you just avoid that person?" asked an amused voice.

"I—I can't, no. There's a long history here, and I..." He floundered, not knowing how to explain he could not be seen by the one person on earth he most wanted to see.

The clerk sighed. "Well. If you haven't done anything in the room, taken anything from the fridge or showered, I guess we can cancel your reservation."

Duff looked at the damp towel he had thrown on the bed. "Well... uh, I did take a shower."

"Then we can't do that, Mr. Duffy. You can leave, but we'll still have to charge you."

He gave up. "Okay, I'll stay. Thank you for your courtesy."

He hung up and looked around the small but cozy room. How he would love a dip in the pool, but he knew that was the first place the girls would head to. He was a prisoner in his room until he could leave early in the morning, hopefully before they ever saw the dawn of day. And him.

He took a seat by the window, making sure the drapes were drawn shut, and leafed through the assorted menus from the restaurants which would deliver meals to his room.

He decided on pizza, made the call, and settled back with a plastic glass of one of the imported beers he liked, which he had picked up in Savannah and brought along with him. He opened the newspapers and began to leaf through the pages, stopping here and there to read articles that interested him.

He didn't see anything cultural happening in the area that night that he might sneak out and enjoy. He thought about his car, and was glad he had hidden in the back of the lot. First sensible thing he'd done about this situation in a long time. The girls not only wouldn't go back there, they probably wouldn't give the car a second glance anyway. But it did have Florida plates. That might attract their attention.

His pizza arrived, and he dug into that, still absorbing northern South Carolina news along with that of southern North Carolina. When he came up for air again, he glanced out the window where he had an oblique view of the pool, and saw that Raina and Marisol had returned, changed into their suits, and were sitting on the edge of the tile, talking.

He snapped the curtain closed. He would not, would not take advantage of the situation to spy on her. But Fate seemed to be placing him everywhere she was, or was it the other way around? Were Raina and Marisol directed to the same places he was so that he might protect them, if the need arose?

She'll be fine.

It wasn't a voice, it was a feeling, but the words were as clear as if they had been spoken. And, he knew whose voice it was.

"Thanks, Granny." He sighed, but he'd made up his mind. Tomorrow he'd head off by himself to Washington. It was another day's drive, and there were things he'd really like to see and do there. He'd much prefer to do them with Raina, but she had a right to her own life, her own likes and dislikes...and just maybe it was up to him to meet her half-way, not insist that she go along with him all the time.

McDonald's wasn't all bad. They had even introduced some salads and healthy foods. It wouldn't kill him to compromise and eat there with her once in a while.

~ * ~

In the dim, overcast morning, he waved goodbye to Marisol's red car and set out for the nation's capital.

He listened to the rest of the Patterson novel, then put in Nelson DeMille's latest thriller. He didn't know which of the two he liked better, but they were both good writers, both told an interest-catching story. And it passed the time.

It took five hours to get through North Carolina. At lunch time he took an exit, which led into a charming, sleepy little town, and he spotted a tiny restaurant that called itself The Best Little Restaurant in the Old South.

He found it totally charming, and after a sumptuous lunch, he wandered into the small antique shop attached to the back.

"Should I pick up something for Raina?" He said the words aloud, not realizing he had.

A tinkling laugh alerted him to the presence of a tiny old lady sitting quietly in a rocking chair in a corner of the shop. He hadn't even noticed her. She looked like an elf, with a wrinkled face, a shock of reddish hair and bright blue eyes that regarded him with amusement. "May I help you find something for Raina?"

Embarrassed, he stammered, "Oh, I'll just look around. Thanks."

The giggle again. "Don't feel funny about talking to yourself. I do it, too, and I'm never lonely, because I have myself to talk to."

Duff laughed because he couldn't help it. "That's true. I'll let you know if I find anything."

He wandered about the shop, which had an amazing variety of charming items. He picked up a gold charm bracelet, put it back again. Raina had dozens of bracelets when she chose to wear them. An old book of photographs of South Carolina in the old days, turn of the century and before, caught his eye. The pictures were all black and white; she probably wouldn't appreciate that. He picked up another book, *Capturing the New South: Landscapes*. He opened to a page at random, then looked at a few of the other photographs. The pictures were spectacularly beautiful, almost a competitor for Ansel Adams, he thought. He flipped back to the cover to see who this remarkable photographer was. He had to take a step backwards, then caught at the counter to keep his balance. It couldn't be...it just couldn't be. But it was. He held a book of photographs by Myrtle Simmons.

"I believe that one's autographed," Rocking Chair Elf called from her corner.

He opened to the cover page, and there was her signature in a generous scrawl. He turned to the back of the book. There was her picture, the woman who had taken him to dinner at an exclusive French restaurant. He could hardly believe his eyes.

He turned to the woman. "I'll take this." He still couldn't comprehend his amazing luck.

"Don't you want to know how much it is?"

"I don't care," he said, and he didn't.

"Now, how about Raina?" the elf asked.

"I—I'll think about that later," Duff stammered. "I can't think about anything else right now."

He paid the woman and escaped from the shop, clutching the precious book under his arm.

On the road again, the hours flew by. Soon he entered Virginia. The sign for Natural Bridge intrigued him, and he veered out of his way to investigate. As he parked the car, he began to worry about the Myrtle Simmons book. He'd had such awful luck; his suitcase with all his clothing and his laptop had been stolen. He'd had to buy an emergency new wardrobe at Goodwill.

And you wound up with better clothes than you had before.

Granny Victoria—right on his case again.

Yeah, well, okay, he argued with himself. *But then I got caught for hours on that bridge between the island and St. Augustine and never got to the movie I wanted to see.*

He felt amusement in the air. *You went to dinner with Myrtle Simmons.*

Mentally, he threw up his hands. "Okay, things happen for a reason, and usually for the best. I don't even want to get into what happened at the truck stop."

She heard you, Duff.

Shock ran all through him, and he shook his head to clear it. Okay, talking to himself was one thing, hearing someone answer him and actually use his name was quite another.

He shoved Myrtle's book under the seat, jumped out of the car and started off on the tourist walk.

Natural Bridge was a rock formation that rose high in the air, and the highway ran right over it. It was a natural bridge, interesting and very picturesque. He walked along the tourist trail, and began to take pictures of the outcroppings and sculptural images on the way. There were several interesting caverns, and he investigated those too.

Nothing strange happened there, for which he was grateful. He got back in his car, rescued the Simmons book from under the seat and put it beside him on the passenger side with Sleeping Beauty. He felt as though he had lots of good company for his trip.

He reached the edges of DC in late afternoon, circled the city on 495, picked a Best Western at random, and checked in. He changed into his swim suit, and taking the book of Myrtle's photographs, the plastic glass from the bathroom, and a bottle of white wine, went down to the pool. After cooling off and swimming laps, he relaxed at one of the tables, and poured himself a glass of wine.

For the first time on the whole trip, he felt relaxed and at peace. He wished Raina were with him, but he was okay alone. He didn't know why, but somehow he knew Raina would be fine, just fine. He'd see her back at the office when the two weeks were up. And when the break-up with Tanya was finalized. And when he had secured his position at Simon's Rock—he hoped—then he'd be free to pop the question.

If he looked at it that way, life could hardly be better.

Twenty-eight

"Where should we go next?"

Raina fastened her seat belt, looked at Marisol and shrugged. "I don't know...why don't we just keep going north and see what we see?"

Marisol pulled the car out of the lot, and out onto the interstate. "Here we go again!"

"Okay." Raina leafed through the stack of tourist brochures. "There are things we could see, but nothing really catches my eye. Do we have time to go to Washington before we head back? I've never been there." She glanced out the car window, watching the minimal scenery flash back. "I guess I've never been much of anywhere."

"Aha!"

Raina turned toward her. "What do you mean, 'aha'?"

Marisol grinned at her. "Just that you're finally realizing that there's more to life than the one you're living in Florida. You've had a tiny taste of it on our road trip, and now something inside you is saying you want more."

"...uhm, maybe."

"Hasn't anything I've said gotten through to you, Raina?"

"Oh, don't get serious on me again, Marisol. I've thought about it...and I think you might be right. I should give Duff more of a chance. I am fond of him. I haven't really been fair."

"Are you attracted to him physically? That's important, too."

"That's another thing." Raina twirled her emerald ring, as she tried to articulate her feelings. "He's been so much of a gentleman, never pushed me any further than I wanted to go. We haven't slept together, you know—I didn't want to encourage him in that way, but—"

"But what?"

"Sometimes, well, it's been hard to stop. I do like him physically, but I thought maybe it was just that I was ready for sex and really wanted it, but he wasn't the right guy."

"Personal question, but—do you ever fantasize about doing it with him?"

"That is too personal...but yeah, yes I do."

Marisol nodded. "Something to think about. If the physical attraction is there, and you enjoy being with him, if you really like him as a person, well, Raina, I do think that's what they call 'love'."

"You mean I've been in love with him and never knew it? That doesn't sound logical to me."

"Because you were fighting it so hard. Just relax, try to forget all your preconceived ideas about the guy. He's a catch, Raina. Think about grabbing the golden ring instead of letting someone else grab it."

Raina nodded slowly and resumed watching the non-scenery go by.

Marisol put the radio on, and Raina listened to the country music with half an ear, tapping out the rhythm on her knee, but thinking about Duff. Was Marisol right? Had she fallen in love with Michael Duffy without even knowing it? Could she build a life with him? Should she?

She was so caught up in her thoughts that she didn't hear the first time Marisol mentioned a stop for lunch. "What?"

"I said where do you want to stop, McDonald's or Burger King? Both coming up on the next exit."

Raina took a deep breath. "Neither. Let's find a good restaurant and have something besides fast-food."

Marisol shot her a raised-eyebrows glance. "Suits me. We'll get off and look for a place."

They drove slowly along the pretty village street. After they passed the fast-food places, there didn't seem to be any other places to eat. As the stores and shops began to ease off, however, Marisol suddenly slowed even more, and pointed. "There's a place—The Best Little Restaurant in the Old South. Want to stop there?"

Raina laughed. "That might be a little too much for me at this point. I'll have to work up to best food. But there's a seafood place, down the street. Crab cakes—yum, let's go there."

"You bet," her friend said and drove into the parking lot.

As they got out of the car, Raina looked around. "What a sweet little town. Too bad Duff isn't here. I bet he'd love this."

Marisol chuckled. "And what do you want to bet we'd find him at The Best Little Restaurant in the Old South?"

~ * ~

They saw the signs for Natural Bridge, but decided to skip veering off the interstate to see it.

"You know," Marisol said. "We can go to DC and spend a couple of days, but we're eating up Tuesday on the road, and we have to figure a couple days to get back home, and it will be pretty much straight driving."

Raina nodded. "I was thinking about that. Is there another way we could get back without taking ninety-five again?"

"Well, we could meander down Route One. We could veer off and go out to Hiltonhead."

"An island in the ocean?" Raina scoffed. "We have plenty of those in Florida, both sides of the coast. What about if we cut over west and go down?"

"That I don't know. Veer over toward Atlanta, I guess, and into the Florida Panhandle. I've heard that's way different from south Florida where we live. We'll have to get a map and check it out."

"Let's pick one up when we stop for gas." Raina suppressed a giggle. "I'll buy."

"The map or the gas?"

"The map. It's your turn to buy gas, but I'll even spring for frozen yogurt for both of us."

Marisol smiled. "You're on."

They stopped in Alexandria, Virginia, at a motel close to the water. The Potomac was alive with boats of all shapes and sizes, sails billowing in the breeze.

"This is awesome," Raina said, looking around. "The architecture's so different in the North. Everything looks so different. I never realized that."

"This isn't exactly the North," Marisol said. "But yes, no one-story buildings without basements, no red-tiled roofs, no Banyons or live oaks."

"Gosh, there's so much I don't know." She looked out over the water. "And there's so much I never wanted to know."

Marisol began to walk along the waterfront. "Let's go find a place for dinner."

"Real food?" Raina asked, hiding a smile.

Marisol nodded. "You bet. Someplace Michael Duffy would want to eat."

~ * ~

Wednesday and Thursday passed in a foggy haze. Marisol had visited the Capitol before and took the lead in showing Raina around.

They walked the mall, stopped at the Vietnam Memorial, said hello to Lincoln seated on his pedestal, and climbed up the Washington Monument.

The White House left Raina breathless. They stood outside the iron fence and gazed across the lawn at the white mansion.

"It's—it's just not the same seeing it in pictures or on TV," she said. "Being here brings it all to life. When I think of all the great men who lived here, it makes me want to go back and read my high school history books."

Marisol grasped the fence and pretended to swoon. "Oooh, of all the things I never thought I'd hear you say!"

Raina nodded, and added thoughtfully. "Maybe there'll be a great woman living there someday.

"Let's hope so."

Thursday morning, Marisol asked over breakfast, "Would you like to tour the National Gallery of Art today?"

Raina, about to reply with her automatic 'no' when asked about visiting art galleries, suddenly thought better of it.

"We're only here once. Sure, I'll give it a try."

They took one of the frequent buses into the city and walked the short distance to the National Gallery where it left them off.

Raina gazed up at the impressive building. Long and low, with a center dome and Greek columns on either side, it seemed to stretch for blocks. "Wait 'til I tell Duff I was here!"

They spent most of the day there, eating lunch in the gallery restaurant, and, realizing they could never see in one day what the place had to offer, wandered at last into the great sculpture garden attached to the west end.

"Wow!" Raina said, as she sank down on one the benches to rest. "And I thought the Norton had a big collection."

Marisol smiled at her. "But, isn't it interesting how much you knew about some of the paintings and the artists that you didn't even realize you knew? Duff has done a great job of educating you about art."

"I guess he has. Yeah, I recognized the Monet, the Chagall, the Kandinsky—and I didn't think I knew one from the other." To her surprise, her eyes misted over. "I owe him so much, and I didn't even know it!"

"Hey!" Marisol dug out a tissue and handed it to her. "Don't go all soppy on me now."

"I—I'm just now beginning to realize how much I almost lost." Another thought struck her. "He told me he had gone with this girl named Tanya from the end of high school all through college, and everyone expected them to get married. What if he goes back to Stockbridge, runs into her and..."

Marisol put her arm around her friend. "Oh, don't start imagining a problem where none exists."

"But it could happen! I've brushed him off so often, maybe he thinks there's no chance with me."

"Raina, get hold of yourself. Let's look at some of the sculptures, then go back to the gift shop. Maybe you could pick some arty little thing for Duff there. That would mean a lot to him."

Raina blew her nose and tucked the tissue into her pocket. "Good idea."

After the long trek back to the Gallery gift shop, Raina was more than willing to call it a day.

"No Kennedy Center tonight?" Marisol teased.

"No! Motel pool, dinner, pool again and bed."

"And tomorrow, on the road, heading home. What are you going to get for Duff?"

"Well, I was looking at the note cards—but who sends notes anymore? I'm thinking, maybe one of these ties. Look, here's an Esher motif, blue with white birds."

Marisol fingered a gold and red print tie. "This one is supposed to be a Kandinsky print. Even I know he's nuts about Kandinsky. Here's another one—how about this one?"

Raina looked at it. It was blue with white circles, and more expensive than the other ties. "Yes! I'll get this one."

As the clerk took the money and arranged the tie in a gift box, Marisol gave Raina a poke in the arm and a sly glance. "Do you think he'll like this as well as the key chain from Clem's?"

Twenty-nine

Duff had circled DC and taken the Silver Spring exit, where he checked into a motel. He remembered seeing a highlight on the food channel about a small market on the main route that had exceptional, home-made treats. Although he didn't admit it to many people, he loved *Chopped*, a program where four executive chefs were pitted against each other and given 'mystery baskets' of outrageous ingredients with which to make an appetizer, an entrée and a dessert. He loved to cook, another legacy from Granny Victoria.

"Makes me wonder what I could do with eel, cucumbers, purple cauliflower and peanut butter." Somehow, those chefs always seemed to make it work.

He put on the brakes just in time to avoid being trapped at the next light. He recognized the storefront from the pictures on TV. He swerved, nearly missing a bright green Jeep whose driver honked the horn angrily at him.

"Sorry, Buddy. Gourmet food calling."

Inside the small shop, the aromas were nearly enough to send him over the edge. The deep-fried chicken looked like it would put Kentucky Fried to shame, if set side by side.

"Bet Thiebault would love to paint you," he murmured to the desserts.

He moved on to admire the side dishes, which all looked one better than the other.

"You'll have to try our turkey and brie turnovers," said the African-American hostess who came out to greet him. "That's what we're famous for, and you have never tasted anything like them, ever." She held out a platter. "Have a sample. Try the chicken, too."

He took a sample of the flaky, orange-glazed turnover and put it in his mouth.

He shook his head at her. "There are no words for this."

She threw back her head and gave a hearty laugh. "That's what they all say. Try the chicken?"

He did, and that, too, was better than any chicken he'd ever eaten. "Are you sure I haven't died and gone to food-heaven?"

That made her laugh again. "Would you like to eat here—" she gestured at a few tables lined up at the side of the shop, "or would you like to take your food to go?"

"I'll take it to go."

On the way back to his motel, he stopped for a copy of the *Washington Post*, and a bottle of white wine, paying twice what he usually paid for wine. But this food deserved the best he could afford.

In his room, he wished he had sprung for some kind of fancy glass to drink the wine from. The plain, solid water glass from the bathroom hardly seemed worthy of such a wine as he had bought.

As he ate the turnovers and the chicken, slowly relishing each bite, he wondered if anyone ever had an orgasm from eating food this good. When he finished his assortment of entrees, he stared at the dense chocolate cake, and wondered how that could surpass what he had already eaten.

He looked at the white plastic fork. This cake looked like it deserved sterling silver, and he was sure it would taste that way, too.

When he had finished, he sat back and shook his head at the empty paper plate.

"Not sterling silver," he said. "That cake should have had a fork of solid gold."

~ * ~

He meant to call Raina, but the wine, combined with his sumptuous feast, made him feel sleepy, and he woke sprawled on of the two queen-sized beds, when his phone rang.

It took him a minute to figure out where he was, and another to locate his phone.

"Hi, Raina! I was going to call you. Where are you?"

"In Alexandria. Oh, Duff, we had such an awesome day. I can't wait to tell you about it."

He took the phone from his ear and stared at it. Was he having a dream? This was Raina, saying she couldn't wait to tell him about her day?"

He put it back to his ear. "What did you do? I don't suppose you visited the riverfront there? It's historic—oh, sorry, I forgot you don't like history."

Her voice rose and fell with a lilt he'd never heard before. "Our motel is right on the riverfront, and we walked along it and Marisol knew about the architecture and told me what the windows and the columns and things were called..."

She rattled on, and he couldn't believe his ears. She actually sounded excited, about the architecture, the history, the river. He felt as though he needed to lie down, but he was already lying down. He listened to her with increasing amazement.

"And, Duff, we walked by the White House, and it almost made me cry, just to be there in person, and realize that all those people in the history books had actually lived there..."

Since he couldn't lie down any further, Duff sat up. He looked at his own dazed expression in the mirror across from him.

"Is this Raina Hudson?" he asked.

He heard her laugh, and it was like a tinkling brook. "Yes, but I think it's a Raina Hudson who awakened. You won't even know her when you get back to the office."

He shook his head. "Don't change too much. I like you just the way you are."

"You can sing that to me sometime," she quipped. "I bet you have a good voice."

Back to Clem's. "Not bad," he said.

She started up again. "We spent all day in the National Gallery," she bubbled on. "And, Duff, I knew so much about the art—so much of it, just from what you've told me. Now I can't wait to learn more. Where can we go when we get back to West Palm?"

"Now I know this isn't Raina Hudson," he said.

"Yes, it is," she said, tinkling her laugh again. "And I bought you a present at the Gallery. Can't wait to give it to you. We're heading back tomorrow, just driving straight down ninety-five. When are you going back?"

"Raina—" he choked. He wanted to blurt out the truth, that he'd been with them all the way, visited many of the same places.

Fate again intervened.

"Oops, Marisol's after me. We're going out for dinner. We saw a Thai restaurant and thought we'd try that. Then we're going to take a boat ride on the river. Gotta go! Talk to you later. Bye, Duff."

"Raina—wait!" But she was gone.

Duff sat for a good twenty minutes, his long legs hanging over the side of the bed, his head in his hands, trying to figure out what he had just heard. Had he had some kind of delusional experience due to the wine and ultra-rich food he'd consumed? Was it based on wishful thinking on his part? Raina, his quiet, controlled Raina, was bubbly-excited over architecture, history, art—and foreign food?

It was too much to believe. He needed another glass of wine. And another.

The next morning, still amazed and bewildered by what had happened the night before, Duff made the motel-provided coffee and tried to concentrate on reading the *Post* from the day before. After a few attempts, he threw it aside.

"Two more days to sightsee before I head for Maine, and all the things, pleasant and unpleasant, that have to be done there. I'm here at the nation's capital, and I should take advantage of that, don't you think?"

The mirror image nodded.

"Besides," he added. "I didn't buy her a present. I just bought myself one."

The mirrored Duff nodded in agreement.

After a minute of staring at himself, Duff asked, "What do you think happened to her?"

The other Duff shrugged.

"C'mon, you're a bright guy. What the hell happened?"

He threw up his hands and yelled "I don't know!"

He sighed. "I planned to 'do' DC today and tomorrow anyway. I'd better get off my duff"—he chuckled at his own joke—"and do that, and see if I can find something I think she'd like. Maybe at the American Indian Museum."

Yeah. How about a feathered headdress? She'd love that.

He intended to go into the city. He loved Washington, the feel of it, the sense of being in the nation's capital. He had only gone a few blocks, however, when he saw a billboard advertising an exhibit at a local gallery in Silver Spring.

"The Gees Bend quilts," he exclaimed, feeling his excitement rise. "I have to see them, I just have to."

Because he had almost reached the 495 exit, he had a hard time finding a place to get off the road and turn around, but he managed it, and headed back to the center of town.

The quilts were every bit as amazing as he hoped. He had read about those phenomenal black women from a rural town in Alabama, with a legacy of quilt-making, who, somehow, without knowing a thing about it, chimed right into the abstract expressionism mode of the sixties, with their homemade quilts. They used the fabrics they had at hand, old clothes, jeans, coats, housedresses—and produced genius.

He walked almost reverently from one room to another, moved as he always was when confronted with the fruits of human talent and imagination.

He turned abruptly when he heard a commotion behind him. A group of school children, all black or mixed race, perhaps a few Latinos, came into the room, with two teachers, one African-American, and one white.

"These are the quilts," one of women said, waving her hand around to indicate the room. She looked as disinterested as did the students.

"So what's so great about these?" the other teacher commented. "My grandmother makes prettier quilts than these."

"Yeah, this is a stupid waste of a field trip, if you ask me."

"When can we go to McDonald's?" asked one of the little girls.

Duff couldn't contain himself. "That's not the point, not the point at all!"

"Oh, do you make quilts?" the white woman asked, sarcasm dripping from her lips.

"No, but I know about these quilts. You do these kids a big disservice if you don't tell them about them. It's their legacy, something to be proud of."

She shrugged, and the other woman joined her, staring at him, with a none too friendly an expression.

"They don't look like so much to me," she said. She glanced around at them. "They're all worn-out looking. Who'd want this old stuff?"

The children crowded around, grinning and poking each other at the confrontation in making.

"Look," Duff said, struggling to explain. "I'm a teacher, and I teach about art. May I please take these kids through and tell them what these quilts really mean?"

The women looked at each other. The one who had led the children into the room shrugged. "Go ahead. Might as well get something back for the money we had to pay for this trip."

He beckoned the children over to look at one of the quilts. "What do you see here?" he asked.

"Ragged old squares," said one of the bigger boys, a handsome kid with a lot of hair and big eyes. "Anybody can make a square."

Duff smiled at him. "Do you know what houses look like in the South? Do they have pointed roofs like the house you live in?"

A pretty little girl wearing jeans and a peasant blouse spoke up. "No! The roofs are flat in the South. We visited my cousins in Florida, and their house has a flat roof."

Duff nodded. "Well, the ladies who made these quilts lived in Alabama, which is right next to Florida."

"So what?" the second teacher-lady asked. "They're still boring. I like crazy quilts better."

Duff ignored her and went on. "If you're a bird and you're flying over a lot of houses with flat roofs, what would it look like?"

There was a silence, then a chorus of "Ohhhhs."

"Like that," the little girl said,

"Exactly. Now come over here. What do you think these shapes look like?" He traced a sequence of parallel rectangles with his finger, moving his hand upward into the air as he did so."

"Stairs?"

"That's right. Now let me tell you about the quilters themselves, and why these quilts are more than just quilts. They are art, and they're part of your heritage."

He took them through the three rooms where the quilts were displayed, and the class followed him, nodding and smiling as he told the story.

He finished, and the black teacher, obviously moved herself, thanked him. "I just didn't know about this. We were told to make this field trip, but nobody gave us any background. I just can't thank you enough."

"You're a good teacher," said the other woman, as she extended her hand to him.

"You taught us something this day," said her companion, as she extended her hand to him.

"I'm not a teacher yet," he said, embarrassed. "But I hope I will be."

He followed the children out.

The little girl in the peasant blouse, trailing the rest of the crowd, turned and winked at him. "You'll be a g-r-e-a-t teacher!" She ran off to join the rest of the class.

No compliment had ever made Michael Duffy happier than that one.

~ * ~

Duff, still feeling elated from his impromptu art-history class on the Gees Bend quilts, took the following day slowly. He visited the American Indian Museum, which he had never seen, and was again moved by the simple elegance of Native American art. The pottery, the blankets, the jewelry, everything spoke to his feelings.

"Maybe Raina would like something from the gift shop here."

"I'm sure she would," a voice replied, and again, he turned to see who had overheard him, embarrassed that he had spoken out loud. Maybe, he thought, this was a habit he should try a little harder to break. But—when you lived alone in a second floor rented condo you got used to voicing your feelings to yourself, or talking back to the TV. How many times had he argued with the political pundits on the telly?

"We have really nice things in the gift shop," she said with a smile. "She put out her hand. "Hi, I'm Sandra. I work here, and I was just heading for the shop myself."

"I'm Duff," he said, shaking her hand.

He liked her looks. She was tiny and compact, probably in her late thirties or early forties. She had a pretty face, a great, friendly smile, and a head of brown hair that twisted and curled around her face and looked like it didn't like being told what to do.

He walked along with her, and found it easy to chat with her. She asked where he was from, and he told her South Florida, but that he'd had to go home to Stockbridge to tie up a few loose ends.

"Stockbridge, Massachusetts?" she asked. "That's where the Norman Rockwell museum is."

"Right," he said, surprised.

She laughed at his expression. "I've worked for the Smithsonian for years. I know where almost every art gallery and museum is."

"Wow," he said. "I'm hoping to teach art history at the college level. I'm waiting to hear from half a dozen places."

She nodded. "I love working in the art field. I'm not an artist myself, though I do knit and make some jewelry."

"That's art," he said. "Everything that's an expression of our inner selves or a comment on the outer world, is art."

She smiled, "That's a pretty wide definition. Covers almost everything."

In the gift shop, he looked around without finding anything that said 'Raina' to him. "Perhaps a book," he mused, although careful to keep his voice inaudible.

He looked at the pottery. It was beautiful, but pricey, and it might break during the flight home. Too chancy. He looked at the jewelry, silver and turquoise, simple and elegant. But—was it Raina? She wore very little jewelry, and this might be too much for her. Maybe a print? There were some of horses running, horses on the beach, horses rearing, their forelegs in the air—but again, nothing called to him.

No, but he felt a little desperate. Raina had something for him, but he had nothing for her. He'd have to look elsewhere. He turned and waved to Sandra, who was leafing through a book, and she returned the wave. As he reached the door, he heard a voice.

Sleeping Beauty.

"What?" He spun around, and that's when he saw it.

A small weaving was displayed with a few others on the wall of the shop. Simple and unaffected, it hung from a curved white birch branch. Its colors were muted, blue and gray and ivory and a touch of soft yellow. He looked at the tag hanging off it. It said 'Sleeping Beauty.' Right away, he knew Raina would love it.

And then, he thought, smiling to himself, he and Raina would each have a Sleeping Beauty to remind them of their separate, but remarkably similar, road trips.

On the way back to the motel, feeling contented and happy, his cell phone rang. Uh oh, impossible to answer it in this traffic. But a little prickle in his neck and arms, intuition maybe, told him this wasn't just any phone call. He saw an exit a half mile ahead, veered over to the right, and took it.

Sitting safely in a shopping center parking lot, he checked his phone. The call had been from his mother, and she had left a message to call her immediately.

"Mom, what's the matter?"

Her voice was choked with emotion. "Duff, I don't know how to tell you this—I know how close you were to her, and—"

He could barely understand her as her sobs muffled her words, as if a dense fog had suddenly fallen between them.

"Mom! For heaven's sake, what is it? What's happened?"

"My mother—Granny Victoria—she died last night." Her words, spaced as if she could hardly get them out, hit him like individual bullets in the chest.

"What?" His head swam. "Granny Victoria died? You're not talking about the one in Maine? Aren't you in Maine? I already know about that—you said no need to hurry." His words jumbled and fell over one another. He didn't know what he was saying.

"No, my mom, Michael. I drove home just last night because she called and said she wasn't feeling well. I told her to check herself out at one of those emergency clinics, but she said no, she'd wait for me. I did see her late last night, and brought her home with me. But this morning when I looked in on her—" Her voice broke again, and the sobs took over.

"And what, Mom?" He could hardly breathe.

"I called out to her and she didn't answer. I went over to her—she just looked like she was sleeping, but there was no pulse..."

"Oh, Mom, how awful." Duff collapsed against the steering wheel. Granny Victoria's face, regal and pretty even in her seventies, filled his vision. She was smiling.

"One thing I have to say," his mother went on, "was that she looked very peaceful, just lying in bed asleep. I think she didn't feel a thing."

Duff sat up and swiped at the threatening tears. "Mom? I'm on the outskirts of DC. I'll leave right now. I'll be home in five or six hours if I don't run into problems. Have to check out of the motel and get my stuff, but I'm on the way."

"Hurry, but be careful," his mother said, her voice breaking. "I don't want to lose you, too. I need you right now. The wake, the funeral, the service—there's so much that has to be taken care of. I just can't believe I have to do this all over again."

"Just hold on," Duff assured her. "I'll be there as soon as I can."

Back on the road in less than an hour, his mother's words rang in his head. There's so much that has to be taken care of.

He nodded to himself. There's something else that has to be taken care of, too. Tanya.

Thirty

He pulled into the driveway of the familiar old house about ten that evening, exhausted both physically and mentally.

The house looked the same, clean and comfortable, but certainly not a showplace. His mother had excellent taste, but nothing was ostentatious. The antiques had been acquired over the years with careful budgeting. He knew that anything of real value that she possessed she had saved for and bought with utmost care. That went for the Oriental vase that sat on the coffee table, and the two Chagall lithos on the wall.

It had been hours since he'd eaten. His mom, after a long, tearful embrace, made him a roast beef sandwich, and set it on a tray with a glass of iced tea and several chocolate chip cookies, which looked and smelled homemade.

He sat on the sofa in the living room, across from one of the Chagalls and ate, while she watched him, occasionally wringing her hands.

"Two deaths in a row, "she said. 'This is so hard, just so hard. I'm so glad you're here."

"I wish I'd been here sooner," he said, blaming himself for not flying up in the first place. Surely his car could have been given to some charitable organization in Florida, and he could have driven the new car back. "I can't believe I'm never going to see Granny Victoria again."

His mother sat back in her chair. He thought her still a handsome woman, but her hair had turned all gray, and it wasn't that pretty silver color that some women were fortunate enough to inherit; it was an iron gray, not particularly attractive.

There were lines etched in her face that he didn't remember, and she looked tired. She wiped away the tears than ran down her cheeks.

Well, of course she looks tired, you idiot! Her mother just died, and you weren't even here for her when she needed you.

"Let's just talk tonight," she said. "Tomorrow is time enough to deal with all the sad affairs we have to take care of. Tell me what the three of you did on your vacation so far—before I had to interrupt you."

He reached out to her, stricken with guilt. "Oh, Mom, don't ever think that. I'm here for you, as I should be, and I want to be."

She smiled, slightly mollified. "Tell me, then. What adventures have you had so far?"

"Oh, Mom, not tonight," he protested. "It's late and you look so tired. Tomorrow is soon enough."

"Tomorrow will come too soon," she said sadly. "And I don't want to think about all that right now. Tell me where you've been and what you've done."

He reflected, but all he could picture was Raina's face, and longing to be near her, if not physically with her, filled him with yearning.

He swallowed. Should he pretend they had all been together, to strengthen his claim that Raina was "the one?" Did it make any sense to tell his mother he had spent an entire week trying to avoid them? He decided that being with Raina would help build his case against Tanya, his decision to break up with her. "The first day we just drove up Florida's turnpike. We took an exit off in early afternoon and had a wonderful picnic in a meadow. Very pretty place next to a fruit stand, and an orchard."

"A nice start," she said, smiling again. "What a lovely picture of the three of you I have in my mind. And then?"

He grimaced inwardly, sure that the picture she had was not the same as his. "We went to Disney. Raina had never been," he explained, seeing his mother's puzzled look.

"Did you actually go on rides?"

"Just one. I remember loving the Peter Pan ride when I was a kid, so I went on that one. The rest of the time I sat on a bench and read a book, waiting for the girls."

"Oh, I remember how you loved that ride," she said with a sigh. "You were about six or seven years old, I think, and you told me you could stay on that forever."

He thought of how he had nearly been on that ride forever, or so it seemed. "Well, we only spent one day there. Then we went on to St. Augustine."

"Oh, just a lovely city!"

He nodded. "Our motel was right on the beach."

"And did you just laze around on the beach, or did you go across that marvelous, long bridge into town?"

"Oh, yes," he said. "I'm quite familiar with that bridge. There was a street festival going on in town and the girls had a blast." *Should I tell her about Myrtle Simmons? Would she even believe me?* He took a deep breath and plunged in. "On the day we got there, the girls wanted to go shopping, so I sat down on a bench on the street to wait for them, and I had the most amazing experience."

She listened, her brow furrowed and her mouth slightly open as he related how the shabbily-dressed old woman had conned him into taking her for dinner at an expensive French restaurant, so he thought, and turned out to be the famous photographer, Myrtle Simmons.

She clapped her hands and laughed out loud. "Oh, Michael, that just couldn't be. You'd believe anything."

"She paid for the meal," he insisted, "and the waiter told me that's who she was."

"Look, just look at this," she said. She got up and brought back a copy of *The Berkshire Eagle*. She rustled the paper in front of him, then turned until she found the page she was looking for, and handed it to him. "This is today's paper, Michael. Yesterday she was in New York City, accepting a prize for—well, something or other. You can read it for yourself. Does this look like your old lady?"

He bent over the paper and looked closely at the photograph. The granny look was gone. He saw a picture of an elegant woman chicly dressed in black with a string of pearls, wearing a lacy picture hat. He nodded his head. She was transformed, but he still knew who it was. "Yes, that's definitely Myrtle Simmons."

His mother shook her head, smiling. "Wednesday in St. Augustine, looking like a bag lady, and this weekend in New York City looking like—well, a famous, wealthy woman? Doesn't make sense, Michael."

"There are planes," he said, a bit testily. "She was in St. Augustine visiting her daughter and taking photographs of the ocean. At least, that's what she told me."

His mother raised her hands in surrender. "Okay, let's not argue about it. You had a wonderful dinner experience, and that's an end to it. What after that?"

He winced. No point going into the gas spill, the shopping trip to Goodwill, or what the cop intimated he might be doing when he changed clothes in the car. "We went on to Savannah."

She clasped her hands together. "Oh, one of my favorite Southern cities! So much to do and see there, the gardens, the old homes. You must have loved that."

"We didn't really get around to that. We did have dinner at a wonderful Japanese restaurant...and then, well, the girls wanted to go dancing, so we went to a club called Dominico's and spent most of the evening there."

She sounded disappointed. "Oh, well, that wouldn't have been my choice of what to do." The she brightened as she reached over and laid her forefinger on his knee. "By the way, I have to congratulate you on your appearance. You seem to be better dressed than usual, and you look very nice, Michael."

"Thanks," he said, wondering if he should make Goodwill his regular shopping venue. He continued his story, but not saying much about his talking to the kids and their teachers through the Gees Bend exhibit, or his trip to the American Indian Museum. That could wait. He had a hunch that what his mother really wanted to discuss was Tanya.

"It doesn't sound like a very exciting vacation," his mother remarked after a minute or two. "I guess it's not so bad that I had to drag you away. I would feel guiltier if I thought you were missing wonderful cultural events and such."

"Oh, I'm not. Raina's really not into much of that, but I'm working on her. But whether she's into all those cultural things or not, Mom, this is the girl for me, and I know I'm going to marry her someday."

His mother's eyebrows shot up toward the ceiling. "Well, Michael, I've been meaning to ask you about that. What about Tanya?"

"Tanya and I have been over for some time," he told her. "There's nothing there anymore."

His mother tilted her head as she looked at him. "I don't think she knows that, Michael. I ran into her just yesterday, and she asked when you'd be coming home, and said she couldn't wait to see you." She looked at him with a question in her dark eyes. "She never visited you all these six months in Florida, did she?"

Duff felt uncomfortable, but decided to be honest with her. "She called often, Mom, wanted to fly down, but I put her off. When I met Raina at the office where we both work, I knew there was no room in my heart anymore for Tanya."

She gave him a glance from the corner of her eyes. "That sounds a little too romantic even for you. You and Tanya have known each other such a long time and you're so well-suited to each other. Are you sure you want to throw all that away."

"Yes," Duff said, feeling as though he was never more sure of anything in his whole life. "Tanya and I just drifted apart, but she doesn't realize it yet. I encouraged her to date other guys, and I think she has."

"Maybe, but she still wants you."

Duff shook his head. "It's Raina now and Raina forever."

She sighed. "You must tell me about her. Let me get us some wine, and you can start at the beginning when you first met her and tell me everything."

She left the room, and Duff yawned and glanced at his watch. It was nearly midnight, but he certainly could stay awake long enough to tell his mom about Raina, and he just couldn't wait; sleep could.

While she was in the kitchen, Duff texted Raina a brief message. It was late and he didn't want to disturb her. *I'm telling my mom all about you...*

Thirty-one

After breakfast the next morning, while he was on the phone with Raina, who had returned his call as soon as she woke up and checked her messages, his mother, dressed in black slacks and a lightweight white sweater, beckoned to him. "We have an appointment at the funeral home. We have to go soon," she hissed at him.

He nodded, and made one more attempt to find out what Raina and Marisol would be doing that day.

"I'm just not going to make you feel worse by telling you what a good time we're having. I shouldn't have told you about the National Gallery. I didn't mean to be so insensitive while you're having such a difficult time, and I'm sorry."

"It's okay, Raina. I feel better when you're just you. It gives me something to remember."

The sad, funereal voice again. "I'll be thinking of you, and praying for you. God bless and bye for now."

He clicked off and turned to his mother. "Okay, let's go get this taken care of."

~ * ~

The funeral for Granny Gray was set for Sunday afternoon. Duff struggled through Saturday in a kind of mind-fog, feeling that what he and his mother were doing was eerily familiar. Of course, during his pretend sojourn in Maine, he had only talked about what he was now actually doing.

His mom wanted to know more about Raina.

"How old is she?"

"Twenty-two."

"Just a little younger than you are. What does she look like? Do you have any pictures?"

"About a thousand." He pulled out his wallet, and spilled the photos out on the kitchen table where they were having lunch. "This is Raina at the office." The picture showed a pretty blonde girl looking up in surprise as he snapped an unposed shot of her. There was Raina, laughing, as a group of them met at a local watering hole for a drink on Friday afternoon. Raina leaning up against the door of a Greek restaurant. Raina running on the beach, her hair flying behind her, her slim figure shining in the sun.

"Here's my favorite," he said, and handed her a printed photo already frayed at the edges. It showed Raina and Duff standing in front of a huge Banyon tree, its twisted limbs forming a dancing canopy behind them.

"She's tall," his mother said. "Tanya's petite."

"Five-eight, not too tall for me."

"And pretty, but Tanya's beautiful."

"I think Raina's beautiful. She has a natural beauty."

"And smart?"

"Very, but she doesn't recognize that side of herself. She actually runs that office, but Dianne keeps a tight lid on things, and keeps all the glory for herself, too."

"Did she go to college, Michael?"

"No...but if we get married, I'm going to push her to do it. Part time, if she wants to work, but once she gets into it, she's going to realize what she doesn't know, and that will set her on fire, I hope."

"Her family?"

'Her mother's an LPN, and her dad works at the local factory. She was brought up very blue-collar, but they're honest, hard-working and great people. You'll like them."

"I know I will. I trust your judgment. But, you know, Michael, Tanya Beeman is a remarkable girl. She's started her own business, and she's really doing well. Haven't you two been in touch at all?"

He rubbed his neck, feeling uncomfortable. "We email. She called a few times. I thought she just sort of eased out of our relationship."

"I don't think Tanya thinks that."

He nodded. "I know you always hoped I'd end up with Tanya, but, Mom, Raina is the girl for me. I feel it in every bone in my body. When I look at her, it's as if..." He trailed off, wondering if what he'd been about to say would sound ridiculous to someone like his mother.

She smiled. "Like she's the part of you that was missing all these years, and now you've found it?"

He nodded, feeling his eyes mist over. "Exactly."

She stood up and began to clear the table. He thought he heard a hint of disappointment in her voice. "Then that's the girl for you."

~ * ~

"Oh, darn," Cynthia Duffy said to him late Saturday afternoon, "I wanted to make this cake for the reception after the funeral tomorrow, and I'm out of vanilla. Michael, could you run to the store and pick up a few things for me?"

"Sure," he said, actually glad of an excuse to get out of the house.

"Take the Lexus," she said, "See how it runs."

"I think I'll walk, Mom. I haven't been home in a while, and I want to see how Stockbridge looks to me after all that time in Florida."

He walked the several blocks to the small market that served the neighborhood. He gazed around, appreciating the look of the old town, the pristine architecture of the buildings, the picturesque main street. He wouldn't mind at all returning to New England if a position at a college opened up here.

But what about Raina? Would she go with him, leave her beloved South? He wouldn't go without her.

There were a few people milling about the market. He glanced at the list his mother had given him, and began putting the items into a small carry-by-hand basket. Hmmm, he wondered, as he surveyed the spices. Did his mom want pure vanilla, or would imitation vanilla, at a considerably lower price, suffice?

He felt a tap on his shoulder and heard a familiar voice. "Michael Duffy!"

He turned. It was the one person he didn't want to run into, but he'd known he would see her at the funeral and the reception following at their home afterwards, anyway. There was no way he could avoid her.

Petite and pretty, she wore her shining hair, brown streaked with lighter colors, loose around her shoulders. Her green eyes shone with pleasure at seeing him, but he could see the question in them too. She wore a short navy skirt and a tan and blue striped tee-shirt.

So New England. He steeled himself. "Hi, Tanya."

"I wanted to call so badly, but I had to respect your time with your mom. I know she needs you so much right now, and I wasn't even sure you were home, since I hear from you so seldom now."

In an impulsive gesture, she threw her arms around him, and he did not feel he should be rude enough to push her away. They did have a long history together. He returned her hug, but quickly let go and pulled away from her.

She looked him over. "You look great, Michael," using the name he'd been known by while growing up in Stockbridge. It hadn't been until college that he'd started to be called 'Duff,' a nickname he much preferred.

"I go by Duff now," he said, forcing a smile.

She arched her eyebrows. "Oh, but Michael is my most favorite name. I'm going to stick with that."

He stifled a sigh. This was vintage Tanya. "You're not looking bad yourself," he said.

The eyebrows shot up further as she assumed the pouty expression he remembered all too well. She placed her hands on her hips. "What do you mean, not bad?"

"I mean amazing," Duff amended. "It's just an expression. It means good, not bad." She did look amazing. She had a face like a porcelain doll, perfect in its symmetry. Although both she and Raina were beautiful young women, they were total opposites.

She grabbed his arm. "You have to come say hello to my parents. They'll never forgive me if I don't bring you home."

"You're all coming to our house for the reception tomorrow, aren't you? Can't I see them then?"

"Oh, they'll never get a chance to talk with you with all those other people around. Our house is just around the corner, as you well know. Just come for a few minutes. Did you walk here?"

He nodded, his heart sinking. He knew there was no way he was going to get out of this. He dug his cell phone out of his pocket. "Just let me tell my mom I'll be a little late."

"Oh, that's not necessary. I have my car. We'll just pop in and say 'hi,' then I'll drive you home."

He gave up. "Okay." he grabbed the pure vanilla and added it to the other few items in the basket. She put his arm through his as they proceeded to the check-out.

"You know," she said in her most perky manner, "I missed you, Michael. What happened to us? I want it back. I really wanted to fly down to Florida to visit you but you kept putting me off."

"Uh, not a good idea, Tanya." He gathered his courage and looked squarely at her. He might as well tell her the truth. "I'm sort of in a relationship."

"You can't be," she pouted. "We never broke up. Just because we haven't been in touch a lot doesn't mean anything. We've both been busy, I realize that. We were meant for each other, and you know it, Michael. If you didn't come back and take a job up here, I would have gone after you down there in Florida."

His heart sank. Did she actually mean that? He felt like a fly walking into the proverbial spider's web. Yet, after the long relationship he and Tanya had shared, he did owe her parents the courtesy of a brief call.

Her 'car' was a shiny, brand new looking, silver BMW.

"Wow," he said. "You must be doing well."

"President of Designs Unlimited," she purred. "My own company, and it's really taken off."

"Wonderful," he replied, and he meant it.

"Aren't you proud of me?" she asked, throwing him a coquettish look.

"Very. I always knew you had it in you."

The Beeman house looked just as he remembered it, a small two-story which tried very hard to be more important than it was. The eight feet of stone facing decorating the front had one of those huge, black metal stars attached to it. The Beemans had added bay windows in front, and encircled the yard with a white picket fence. Climbing roses bloomed all over the fence, and in the middle of the front yard stood a stone well that wasn't a real well—just a wooden structure pretending to be one.

Dawn and Joe Beeman welcomed him with real joy. Duff knew they had always hoped he and Tanya would marry. How could he explain that after one year of high school and four years of college, he'd had enough of their aggressive, type A daughter? He'd gone on to get his Master's degree at a university in Florida, while she got right busy establishing herself as a business maven in the community. Already feeling a disconnection from Tanya, he decided to stay in Florida while searching for a permanent position. He had looked for something he could consider a temporary job in the interim, and found the office position in Jupiter.

Dawn held him at arms' length. "Goodness, Michael, you look just wonderful."

"His taste in clothes has improved drastically, too," Tanya added, smiling proudly at him."

You'll stay for dinner, of course," Dawn purred, sounding just like her daughter. "I won't take 'no' for an answer."

Duff shook his head, knowing in advance that his refusal was useless. Dawn, like Tanya, never gave up 'til she got her way.

"I'll call your mother and explain that we just must have you for an hour or so," she said, and headed for the phone.

"Come in, Michael, and have a beer," Joe Beeman insisted. He led the way to the small, immaculate living room which Dawn had furnished with pretend-antiques.

Duff's heart sank. It was all too familiar—too eager Dawn, too-convivial Joe, the grasping Tanya. Not at all like free-spirited Raina.

He felt as if there were a noose around his neck, being pulled tighter and tighter by the minute.

"You come from such a good family," Dawn had cooed to him more than once. More than twice, more than ten times. The not so subtle hint was that she wanted Tanya to be a member of that 'good' family, too.

It totally annoyed Duff to be thought of as a 'prize' that might be awarded to her daughter. Raina's family was not well-off, but they were genuine, and they liked him because he was Duff, not because his family had been well-off, respected and considered 'cultured.' Duff's father had taught painting at the Hartford Art School University of Hartford in West Hartford Connecticut, arranging his classes for three long days in a row, so that he could stay over there, lodging two nights with a friend, home for the rest of the time.

The beer was an imported Greek brand that Duff particularly liked. He felt his irritation grow, and tried to tamp it down. "I see you stuck with this brand of beer. Wasn't I the first to introduce you to it?"

Joe nodded, grinning. "You bet. You always did have good taste." He winked. "In beer, and in girls, too."

Dawn and Tanya joined them. Tanya carried two glasses of wine, one for herself and one for her mom. She sat on the sofa beside him, and laid her hand possessively on his knee.

Dumb, dumb, dumb! Why didn't you sit on a chair?

Duff crossed and recrossed his legs, so that she had to remove her hand, but as soon as he seemed settled, she put it back again.

He sighed. This was going to be one heck of a long hour. He wanted to talk to Raina. He didn't want to be sitting in a former girlfriend's living room with her much too interested parents, having a beer he didn't care about, waiting for a dinner he didn't want.

"When are you coming back here?" Dawn asked. "Tanya's been very lonely without you."

He decided to be direct, even though that would make for an uncomfortable dinner hour. "I need to tell you, Mr. and Mrs. Beeman—"

"Joe and Dawn," Tanya's dad said, beaming at him. "You're like one of the family now."

"And Tanya, too." He set his beer down on the coffee table, which he noted, boasted a copy of *Illus*, a magazine of pretty pictures and corny poems. "That's just the thing, Joe and Dawn. I got a temporary job in Florida—just until I get the college position I really want—and I met a girl there."

Dawn smiled, not getting his message at all. "Oh, can she make a connection for you about a job? Where would that be?"

Duff groaned an inward groan. "No, Dawn, it's not that at all. You see, I fell head over heels in love with her. She's the girl I'm going to marry. Her name is Raina Hudson." As he said her name, he felt as though she had brushed a caress over him.

The temperature in the room seemed to drop thirty degrees, and the silence was like frost on the river.

Tanya snatched her hand from his knee and stared at him in disbelief.

"But...but..." Dawn stammered, turning pale, "you and Tanya have been planning to get married since high school. It's all we wanted for her. You come from such a good family..."

Tanya said stonily, "How can that be, Michael? We never broke up."

He nodded unhappily. "I know we never officially broke up, Tanya, but we didn't see each other at all, except during the holidays last year."

"At which we were still considered a couple," she replied.

"Yes, well..." he limped on. "I just thought we had drifted apart. I didn't hear much from you, and uh..."

"And you didn't get in touch with me either," she said. Her voice was frosty, but her eyes were colder. He shivered, even though the night was warm. "I was busy setting up my business, for us. That BMW you so admired was not all for me, Michael. It's a success symbol I wanted you to share."

He stared at the coffee table. "I'm sorry, Tanya."

"You're sorry! You hardly answered my emails, you never called. And when I called, you had something else you had to do. Was that something else called Raina?"

"Yes." The coffee table had a scratch made by something sharp. He ran a finger over it.

Tanya stood, her face stormy as she glared at him. He knew she was headed for a full-fledged tantrum, and that was something with which he was all too familiar. He didn't care to see another one.

Joe sat in his chair, humped over, hunching his shoulders over and over. He looked as though he'd just buried his best friend.

Dawn had started to cry softly. She wiped her eyes with a tissue, and gave him a pleading look. "Michael, if you'll just take time to think this over. You can't be in love with someone you just met six months ago. Don't give up what you and Tanya have together, please."

Duff stood. "I'm sorry, but I am one hundred percent in love with Raina Hudson. I can't even think about being with someone else now." He drew a deep breath as he looked around at the devastated family. "I think I had better go now." He looked at Tanya, whose face radiated the fury of her hurt. "I never meant to hurt you, but things happen. I guess I'm just not very good at breaking up."

He headed for the door, remembered his manners and turned back to three people staring at him with destroyed expressions on their faces. "It was nice to see you all."

As he fled the house, he heard Tanya screaming, and Dawn's voice trying to calm her. "Now, honey, we'll figure something out. He'll come to his senses."

"No, I won't!" he said aloud as he raced toward home. "Because she said I was driving her crazy and insisted we take a vacation from love, we did that, but for me it's Raina now, Raina tomorrow, and Raina forever after."

It started to sprinkle lightly, a soft, clean, refreshing rain. It felt good on his skin.

"See?" he said, to no one in particular, "Rain! It's a sign." He laughed and folded his hands in a prayer-like attitude. Thank you, Raina. Amen."

Thirty-two

"You look very nice, Michael," his mother said, appraising the navy blazer over the blue and white striped shirt and dark pants he'd bought at Goodwill. "But do put a tie on, will you? And hurry up. We can't be late for the service."

"Uh, I don't have one," he admitted. He'd searched through his second-hand clothes but found no trace of the ties he had bought. He must have lost them at one of the motels.

"You have to wear a tie," she said. "It just looks entirely too casual if you don't. You know how these proper Congregationalists are."

He spread his hands. "I'm sorry, Mom, I just don't have one. Isn't there one of Dad's lying around some place?"

She considered, then turned on her heel. "I don't think so...but maybe. I'll go check."

Five minutes later, she came back holding a tie, with a strange expression on her face. "This is the only one I could find...I know it's not the best choice, but maybe nobody will notice. It's better than no tie at all. Everyone would notice that."

She handed him the tie.

"Mom, I can't wear this!" He looked at the Christmas tie in disbelief. It had an image of Rudolph, padded so that the reindeer stood out from the background, with red sequins for his nose. A wreath of holly surrounded him. Below the wreath, just where the tie would tuck into the jacket, was a green button.

"Don't press the button," his mother said. "It plays 'Rudolph.'"

Duff threw the tie on the table. "I can't wear this. It's July."

"You can't go without a tie," his mother said firmly. She picked it up and handed it back to him. "How about on the other side?"

He turned it over. The reverse side was a vague woven pattern of red and green. "Well…" he said.

"That will do," Cynthia said. She put the tie around his neck, smoothed it beneath his collar, and knotted it expertly, as she had always done for his father. "There," she said. "Nobody looks at ties anyway, and as soon as we're out of the church, you can take it off."

The funeral service took place at Second Congregational Church. It was not a large sanctuary, and the pews were crowded. Duff, seated with his mother and some of her close friends in the first pew, looked around several times to see if the Beemans had even shown up. On the third peek around, he spotted them, on the right side, toward the back. Joe and Dawn smiled at him as if nothing untoward had happened the day before, and Tanya threw him a smile that would melt a stone, and waved.

Oh, oh. He turned back toward the front and sighed. He was in for it. He knew this side of Tanya, too. It was what had made her so successful. Once she made up her mind, she never changed it. And evidently she'd decided she wanted Michael Duffy from the good family. Unfortunately, he no longer wanted her.

It was sort of as if you always ate Hershey bars, and never gave it a thought that there might be something more delectable out there. After all, they were quality chocolate, tasty and took care of that chocolate craving that hit once in a while. But then, once you'd had one f those new concoctions with the Reeses pieces buried in it—well, he didn't think he could ever go back to plain Hershey bars.

He relished that analogy. Tanya was a quality girl, beautiful and smart, no doubt about it, but she lacked something...the complicated layers that made up Raina. He never knew what to expect from her, and he was always surprised when he found out something new about her. Tanya was already all she was going to be; she was a designer rose in full bloom, and some guy would be lucky to win her. But Raina was a vine with a thousand buds that had not yet begun to bloom. When they did, she would be one spectacular woman. And the man who won her would be in for the ride of his life.

The congregation stood for a hymn, something about being in peril on the sea. It was a lovely hymn with an addictive melody, but what did it have to do with Grandma Gray? Maybe the pastor had written her eulogy as an analogy of life being a voyage on the ocean. Something like that.

The minister was young and very earnest. He ascended the pulpit, which was reached by a curving staircase of six or seven steps. On the fourth step, he his robe caught on something, and he was forced to abandon his dignity temporarily, and struggle to free himself. There was a murmur of amusement from the congregation.

His face red, the Reverend Jeremy Brown began his eulogy. He had only been pastor of Second Congregational for a year, and although he had known Victoria Gray, he had not known her well.

His mother leaned into him and whispered into his ear, "He could be talking about anybody."

Duff nodded. It was true. He spoke about the 'quality of her life,' never mentioning whether it was good or bad. He spoke about her legacy (what legacy?) and 'the impact she had made on her children and grandchildren.' (What impact?) And, considering that his mother had been her only child, it was doubtful she'd had an impact on any others. He didn't say a word about the beautiful quilts she'd made and sold, or given away, her impeccable taste, her quirky sense of humor, her service to the local garden club, or something a lot of people didn't know—her fascination with cats, all kinds, from barn cats to lions and cheetahs. She thought they were the most beautiful and interesting animals God had put on the earth. And cats loved her, too. There was never a cat anywhere they visited that did not instantly jump into her lap and refuse to leave.

The church doors had been left open, as it was a humid day, and the breeze that wafted through the non-air-conditioned church was more than welcome. That was a usual practice, with an usher stationed there to ward off any unwelcome visitors. Of course, in a well-bred and rather uptight town like Stockbridge, there never were any.

The usher must have answered a call to go to the men's room, however. The congregation began to titter with amusement as a large, gray and white striped tom cat walked down the aisle with complete confidence. He walked up the steps to the platform where the altar, pulpit and lectern stood. He turned around and gazed at the congregation.

It was the most interesting thing to happen during the service. Pastor Brown looked at the cat, but didn't seem to know what to do and everyone else, charmed, wouldn't have removed the cat for anything. There were three throne-like chairs behind the lectern in the chancel, where the pastor and other dignitaries sat, when there were any. The cat strolled over to one of the chairs, jumped up, turned around, and sat perfectly still like an Egyptian statue, and stared out at the congregation. A few people laughed out loud.

At times, as the pastor continued to speak, the cat turned to look up at Jeremy Brown, and cocked his head as if trying to understand a certain statement. Several times, as the minister paused to make a point, the cat let out a 'meow,' which sounded a lot like 'amen.' At one point, when the Reverend Brown sounded his most serious, the cat lowered his head and shook it from side to side. Can't agree with that, it seemed to say. The laughter from the crowd grew.

The congregation rose for the last hymn, trying hard to control their amusement. But not succeeding very well. Duff noticed a few women wiping tears from their eyes, but he suspected it was from laughing, not from crying.

A soloist rose to sing "Will the Circle Be Unbroken?' and the tittering died away. Even the cat looked pensive, as the haunting words floated over the congregation. Tears replaced the laughter, and Duff felt his own eyes filling. That song was so Grandma Gray, with her tenderness and love of family. She would never want to be separated from them, nor they from her.

The service ended with "Our God, Our Help in Ages Past," and Duff rose to sing it with relief that it would soon be over. But, after the actual burial, which would not take long, there would be the reception at their house to deal with, and the Beemans, including Tanya, would all be there.

The ushers, formally dressed, came forward to carry the closed casket out of the church. As each took his place and raised the coffin, the cat jumped down from the chair and went before them down the aisle. The aisle seemed very narrow, and Duff wondered if it were perhaps too narrow for the casket. But, he reasoned, surely they had had funerals there before, and other caskets had been carried down the same aisle.

They had not gone five steps before one of ushers stumbled, went down on his knee, and the side of the casket crashed into the side of the pew. The woman sitting there jumped, and cried out in alarm. The cat turned around to look, and waited.

The ushers righted themselves, but the one in the lead, an elderly man, seemed to be having a hard time holding up his end of the coffin. Another few steps brought another bump on the other side of the aisle. Again the cat waited.

The congregation tried not to laugh, but they were already warmed by the cat. Several people broke down into open laughter, and others joined. The ushers, mortified, continued to bump their way down the aisle, and at last, mercifully, got out into the narthex.

Duff ushered his mother out of the pew, and stood beside her, waiting to precede the congregation from the church. Nervously, he put his hand to his chest as they waited for the ushers' signal to begin their solemn procession.

The joyous strains of "Rudolph the Red-Nosed Reindeer" rang out, just as the organist stopped playing.

"Ignore it!" His mother took his arm, and they walked with all the dignity they could muster down the aisle.

When Duff and his mother exited the church, the cat was nowhere to be seen.

His mother took his arm. "That was perfect," she said, smiling. "Mom would have loved it."

Thirty-three

Cynthia Duffy was used to mass entertaining, and had hired a number of local high school girls to move among the crowd with offerings of food. The appetizers and canapés came first. She had engaged a caterer also, although most of the serving was done by the young girls. The caterer set up a bar in the corner of the large living room, near the fireplace, and served drinks from there.

Duff and his mother mingled with the guests, accepting their condolences, and laughing with them about the cat who had attended the service. Tanya attached herself to him and acted as if they were a couple, pretending for all the world as if it were her beloved grandmother who had just passed on.

Tanya looked stunning, Duff had to admit, every inch the successful young executive in a chic black dress, a single diamond on a gold chain around her neck. Her creamy skin, set off by that gleaming hair, was flawless. Although short and slim, she had a commanding poise that drew admiring eyes to her. If he loved her...if he just could love her, she would make the perfect wife for a college professor.

Duff sighed. There was just no way. His heart had been captured beyond recall.

Kent Bridges, Duff's casual friend from high school, looking very lawyerly and important in his expensive gray suit, pulled him aside.

"I'll be right back, darling. Just going to get a refill on my wine." Tanya gave him a little wave and headed toward the bar.

Kent grinned at him, and shook his arm. "Hey, you lucky duck! When's the wedding date?"

"There isn't any, Kent. I'm not marrying Tanya."

The lawyer looked incredulous. "You're not? You've gone with her since high school—and look at her. Man! You're a fool if you don't nail that one."

Irritated, Duff shook his head. "Do you see a ring on her finger?"

"Well...I was assuming maybe Christmas. Wedding next summer?"

Duff, tired of trying to be cautious with his explanations, blurted out, "Engagement not at Christmas, not Valentine's Day, not St. Patrick's Day, not Easter...not even April Fool's Day, and wedding never. I don't love her. I met someone else down in Florida."

Kent reeled back, and squinted at Duff, as if interrogating a witness on the stand. "No kidding? She must be something else, if you'd give up Tanya for her. Don't be a fool, Michael, when a hot chick like Tanya is throwing herself at you."

"The other one's...a different type. More natural. Just herself."

Tanya reappeared, slipped between the two men, and looked up at Duff, then back to Kent? "Don't you think I'm a lucky girl, Kent?"

He raised his glass in a salute. "The luckiest, Tanya. You just don't know yet how lucky." He shot Duff a look of scorn and disbelief and turned to speak to someone else.

Tanya raised herself on tiptoe, so that she could whisper something in his ear. He bent down, and the scent of her perfume caught him off guard, tickling his nostrils.

He sneezed.

"Bless you!" several people said.

He sneezed again, then couldn't seem to stop.

He handed his glass to Tanya and fled to the bathroom down the hall, feeling the curious glances that followed him.

In the bathroom the sneezing finally stopped. He leaned against the wall and looked at himself in the mirror. The whole day, from the Rudolph tie to the addition of the cat to the service, to the hitting the sides of the pews with the casket as the bearers exited the church, had been a horror. Yet, he knew his grandmother, always ready with a pun or funny retort on her tongue, would have loved it.

Yes, I loved it!

There was that voice in his head again, and it did sound suspiciously like Granny Gray. He shook himself. He had other things to think about right now.

He had to deal with Tanya. This was something he wasn't looking forward to. With their lack of communication that past year, her preoccupation with her career, his newfound love interest, he had taken it for granted that their relationship was over. He guessed he hadn't paid enough attention to her frequent emails, hadn't read enough between the lines. She still wanted to think they were a couple.

Even though he thought he had made it clear last night, it was obvious she was making one last attempt to hook him in.

"Come over for dinner tomorrow night," she cooed at him at the end of the service. "Just you and me. I make a mean coconut shrimp. Just so succulent, pink and juicy..." her voice trailed off in a meaningful way.

"Well, I—" but she hadn't taken 'no' for an answer. Bidding him and his mother goodbye at the door, she wiggled her fingers at him and blew him a kiss. "See you tomorrow, Michael, about seven."

Okay, he had to reverse the situation, make her break up with him. He checked his watch. By six-thirty the reception dinner would be over, but he couldn't leave his mother alone this evening, of all evenings. But tomorrow...he would solve the Tanya problem once and for all, claim the gorgeous new car his Maine grandmother had left him, head for Florida and finish this disaster of a vacation.

As the last of the guests departed, his mother turned to him with a worried look. "You have a date with for Tanya tomorrow night? Have you given serious reconsideration to breaking up with her? She's a fine young woman, and I always thought you would make a wonderful couple. You'd better think this over carefully, because if you break your date with her, she'll never forgive you."

He grinned. "I'm counting on that."

And he couldn't wait to get back to his boyhood bedroom and call Raina.

Thirty-four

Home was there, just as he had left it, but it seemed emptier than ever. He dropped his new, second-hand suitcase on the floor. With a sigh, he began to leaf through all his accumulated mail. Bills, bills and more bills, and advertisements. However, as he sorted through the envelopes, his eye fell on the Simon's Rock return address. His heart turned a summersault. Oh, please...please let them want me.

They had a spot for an art history teacher. They were interested in his resumè. They would like him to come for an interview. If it all worked out, he would start in the fall.

"Simon's Rock!" He had hardly dared to hope. This was an experimental combination, very trendy private high school and college. He would have the cream of the crop for students, kids who would truly be interested in art and culture.

It sounded almost too good to be true. Back to New England, back to his roots, close to his family in the Berkshires, a beautiful part of the state of Massachusetts. Skiing in the winter, Tanglewood in the summer. Williamstown. Summer theatre. Lakes and streams and mountains. Changing colors in the fall. A perfect place to settle and bring up a family.

But into the ecstasy of his imagination crept a sudden thorn, pricking his joy like a pin deflating a balloon. Raina. Would she go with him?

Without her, he couldn't accept this prize position.

He'd rather work at a carwash, if he could have Raina, than have the most prestigious position he could imagine without her.

He ran his hand over his forehead and his fingers through his hair.

Tomorrow he'd be back at the office, and tomorrow he would know what would decide his fate.

~ * ~

Dianne strode into the office, her back straight as a rod, her heels clicking on the tiled floor.

Oh, how I've missed that! Not.

Her chin, held high, led the way, and the skirt of her black suit swished behind her as she walked.

Duff had just come into the office himself. He'd stretched his neck to see if Raina was in, and he caught a glimpse of her hair in her cubicle. As usual, Marisol was with her.

He could hardly wait to see her, talk to her, hold her in his arms, but he knew that would have to wait. However, as soon as Dianne was shut up in her office, he could go and say hello, at least. He started up his computer, and began to program the work he would do that day. It looked as if the temp had not accomplished much, but that was all right—he could catch up in no time.

Dianne ignored Duff as she passed his cubicle.

"Good morning, Miss. Ryder," he called out, more to annoy her than to be friendly.

She turned her head a fraction of an inch in his direction and raised an index finger. That was it. At least it wasn't the third finger.

She swooped past Raina's station. Not favoring either girl with a glance, she went into her office and closed the door, just a little more forcefully than necessary.

"Guess we're in for it," Duff said cheerfully.

Alan, who worked in the next cubicle, turned and looked back at him. "You have no idea. It's been hell around here."

Duff looked up. "Oh? I thought Raina arranged for a temp, and she was supposed to be good."

'She was good," Alan said "But Dianne came down on her like a ton of bricks and she quit the third day. We weren't able to get anyone else in, so we're way behind."

"I noticed."

Alan cast a quick glance at Dianne's office door, then leaned over and said, with a smirk. "The Great One had to lower herself to come out and do some of the work herself, and even then, I hear she caught it from—Up There." He jerked his head upwards.

"No kidding?"

Duff stood up, intending to go greet Raina and Marisol, but as he stood, Raina appeared before him, a big smile on her face.

"Hi, Duff."

That was all, just two words, but they told him in an instant that his world had changed. She had never come to his cubicle, never in the six-plus months he'd been there.

"Hi," he said, feeling suddenly shy. What was the matter with him?

And why didn't Marisol come with her? They were always joined at the hip. He never got a chance to talk to Raina alone, unless he'd managed to get a date with her.

"Did you have a good road trip?" He wanted to put his arms around her so badly, he had to clasp his hands behind his back to keep himself from doing just that.

"It was awesome." Raina smiled at him again, a softness in her expression he'd never seen.

"Raina—" he began.

"I know," she said.

"You do?"

"I do."

"Those are the words I've always hoped I'd hear you say," he quipped.

"I will."

"You will what?"

"I will say those words at just the right time."

"Will you be wearing white?"

"Yes."

"Will you be carrying flowers?"

"Yes."

"Raina—"

"I know."

The door to Dianne's office opened, and the dictator herself burst out. "Marisol Martinez, Raina Hudson, Michael Duffy! Conference Room Two on the double."

"Here we go again," Duff said.

Marisol joined them, grinning from ear to ear.

"Well?" she asked.

Duff and Raina looked at each other. "Yes," they said together.

She threw her arms around the two of them. "I'm so happy for you," she exclaimed, giving Duff a huge grin.

After a moment, she pulled away. "Well, let's go face the demon."

Dianne sat at the oval table tapping her pen in the table, her face covered with thunderclouds.

Her pale blue eyes flicked shards of ice at each of them in turn. "Well, it's nice to see you all back." Her voice dripped sarcasm. "But we have a situation here, due to all three of you being gone for two weeks, so here's what we're going to do to fix it."

You're going to Simon's Rock. The same voice, the one he'd heard several times. Duff knew he could trust it.

"Mr. Duffy, your replacement was a disaster. You will be working two hours overtime each day for the next month to make up for that. And no overtime pay."

Duff sat back in his chair and looked at her. "I don't think so, Dianne."

She winced at his use of her first name. She always stressed formality as office protocol.

"You don't think so? Then I will fire you, Mr. Duffy."

"Fine with me. Do you want me to finish out the week or not?"

"Excuse me, Mr. Duffy, but do you want this job or not? With the economic situation the way it is, you're going to have a tough time finding a job that pays as well as this one does, for the little work you manage to crank out."

"I'll be leaving the middle of August anyway. I have secured a position teaching at a private school in Massachusetts." Duff kept his voice pleasant, and smiled at her.

Her mouth fell open. For once, she seemed to be speechless.

"If you want me to stay until August, I will. Otherwise, I'll leave at the end of the week." He shrugged. "Or today, if that's what you want. I aim to please."

He glanced at Raina. She held his eyes with hers, and her face still wore the same soft expression.

Dianne looked away from him and turned her venom on Raina. "And you, Miss Hudson, that temp you inflicted on us was worthless. She quit the third day."

Raina smiled and nodded. "I heard."

Dianne tried again. "Therefore, Miss Hudson, you will be working two hours a day overtime also. And no overtime. You owe us this, for the inconvenience you have put us through."

Raina followed Duff's lead. "I don't think so."

Dianne got to her feet and leaned over the table. "Miss Hudson, I warn you, don't oppose me. I'm proud of running a tight ship here, and you will do as I say." She glared at Raina. "You are so incompetent. I have to go over everything you do. Where would a silly little twit like you find another job like this?"

"In Massachusetts," Raina said. "I'm going there when Duff goes. I'll find a job, and it won't matter what it is as long as I'm there with him."

Dianne looked as if she might suffer a stroke on the spot as she looked from Duff to Raina and back again. "Well," she said at last, "if there were ever a mismatched couple, you two are it. But that's not any of my concern."

Duff stopped smiling at Raina and shifted his gaze to Dianne. "No, it isn't."

Dianne sank back down in her seat. Her eyes raked over Marisol. "Miss Martinez, it looks like it's all going to land in your lap. When this odd couple leaves in August, you will take over both of their jobs."

Marisol examined her fingernails. "I don't think so."

Dianne jumped to her feet again. "Don't you dare talk back to me," she yelled. "Just what do you think you have to gain by defying me? Are you going to Massachusetts, too?"

Marisol shook her head. "No, but I am going to be assistant office manager, and get a damn good raise. I've already left a letter with Personnel. They know who does all the work around here."

Dianne looked daggers at all three of them in turn, then turned and walked out of the office. Her back wasn't quite as straight, and her heels didn't click quite so forcefully on the tile.

Marisol smiled at Duff and her best friend. "I think I should leave you two alone for a while. I bet you have a lot to catch up on." She looked at her watch. "As assistant office manager, I'm giving you a half hour break before you need to return to work."

She gave them a wink and left, closing the door behind her.

Duff reached for Raina's hand. "Raina, did you mean what you said? Did I understand you correctly? Will you marry me and move to Massachusetts with me?"

The soft look again that reached straight into his heart. "Massachusetts sounds like a foreign country to me, but yes, I will."

"This is the happiest day of my life," Duff told her, rolling his eyes to the ceiling, before gazing back at her. "Two weeks ago, I thought there wasn't a chance in the world that I would ever win your heart, but I was determined to keep on trying. Then—everything changed. It's a miracle."

"No," she said gently. "Two weeks ago all I wanted was a vacation from you—a vacation from love, I called it, because you really were driving me crazy. But—things happened on this road trip. I had time to think, and when I got my thoughts all in the right order, I realized that I do love you, and I never want a vacation away from you again."

He didn't know what to say. The last two weeks had changed him, too.

"How about dinner at McDonald's and seeing a Jim Carrey movie tonight?" he asked. He would meet her half way.

She cocked her head and looked at him, teasing. "I don't know... did you have the two dates with other women I told you to have before I went out with you again?"

"I did," he said promptly. "One of them was eighty-two years old, and the other was Japanese."

She laughed. "Yeah, I bet. Well, I was thinking El Torrero for something hot and Spanish, and I have tickets for a play at the Maltz afterwards."

"Oh, Raina." He got up and went to her, enfolding her in his arms. He felt something metallic clank against his arm. He glanced down.

He blinked his eyes in disbelief as Raina held out a key chain. He recognized the Clem's logo, and the metal engraving of the truck stop, and again, he felt as if he were in another world, experiencing something that just couldn't be.

"I have another, nicer present for you," she said shyly, "but—well, this is kind of goofy, but we were in a silly mood when I bought it. Anyway, it's sort of symbolic of our trip." She shrugged. "I know you like nicer things. You can just throw it out if you want to."

He drew her closer, breathed in the clean scent of her hair, felt the warmth of her closeness, and knew that whatever had happened to both of them during the past two weeks had joined them together forever. Maybe there'd been a little help from Beyond—Grandma Victoria, maybe. Maybe not. But Raina was his at last, and he was hers, and life just couldn't get any better.

"Raina," he said, "I know I have told you that you're driving me crazy, and you do, in ways you don't even realize."

"Oh, I think I do," she said. "And I intend to keep driving you crazy for the rest of our lives."

"I can live with that," Duff said as he tightened his arms around her.

He bent his head to kiss her, and as his lips met Raina's, Duff knew that somewhere, Granny Victoria was smiling.

Meet Joan Conning Afman

Joan Conning Afman taught art in the Hartford, CT school system for seventeen years before retiring to Florida. Always interested in writing, she found the opportunity and encouragement to do so with a group of new friends in the Sunshine State. She likes to add something in her books about art that might be new to the reader, and also introduce interesting locations. Sometimes another interest of hers, situations that include the paranormal, also find their way into her stories. *Drivin' Me Crazy* incorporates all of these.

Joan has four grown children of whom she is inordinately proud, and six beautiful grandchildren. She keeps busy writing, painting and exhibiting her work, and thoroughly enjoys the social and cultural life of south Florida.

Other Works From The Pen Of
Joan Conning Afman

Sacrifice At Mystery Hills - An ancient site, an eerie rite, and Evil reigns again.

The Last Time We Were Here - Old friends and foes meet again at class reunion.

Letter to Our Readers

Enjoy this book?

You can make a difference

As an independent publisher, Wings ePress, Inc. does not have the financial clout of the large New York Publishers. We can't afford large magazine spreads or subway posters to tell people about our quality books.

But, we do have something much more effective and powerful than ads. We have a large base of loyal readers.

Honest Reviews help bring the attention of new readers to our books.

If you enjoyed this book, we would appreciate it if you would spend a few minutes posting a review on the site where you purchased this book or on the Wings ePress, Inc. webpages at: https://wingsepress.com/

Visit Our Website

For The Full Inventory
Of Quality Books:

Wings ePress.Inc
https://wingsepress.com/

Quality trade paperbacks and downloads
in multiple formats,
in genres ranging from light romantic comedy
to general fiction and horror.
Wings has something for every reader's taste.
Visit the website, then bookmark it.
We add new titles each month!

Wings ePress Inc.

3000 N. Rock Road

Newton, KS 67114